The Sea Queen

Cover Art by Nathalia Sullen
Formatted by D2D
My super seekrit hangout!

This is a work of fiction. All characters, places, and events are from the author's imagination and should not be confused with fact. Any resemblance to persons living or dead, events, or places is purely coincidental. Though if you should spot a cute fairy or a lecherous imp, say hi for me.

Published in 2015 by Jovee Winters, United States of America

The Sea Queen

Calypso, Queen of the Seas, is mad. Spitting mad. Ghosts of the dead are fouling her waters. She wants this problem fixed, and she wants it fixed now. Rushing off in search of Hades, Lord of the Underworld, to demand answers, she's soon shocked to discover him bound and standing trial before a jury of his peers—for nothing less than murder.

Calypso normally despises the beastly gods, all of them, but there's something about seeing Hades bound as he is that gives her an evilly clever idea. Tired of being a virgin queen, she wishes to shed that boring image once and for all, and no one seems quite as fit for the task as the gorgeous and brooding Hades. Of course, there is the minor problem of murder to deal with, but Calypso is bound and determined to have her way.

And when a dark queen gets an idea, nothing and no one can stand in her way...

Dedication

To all the people that I love, you know who you are. And to my Harem, cause there's no place on the web half as fun as you guys!

The Sea Queen

The voice of the sea speaks to the soul. The touch of the sea is sensuous, enfolding the body in its soft close embrace. ~ Kate Chopin

You are not a drop in the ocean. You are an entire ocean in a drop. ~ Rumi

Forward

The Sea Goddess, Calypso. Tempestuous. Alluring. Enticing. Mesmerizing. Ephemeral and yet eternal. She always was and always will be. Born beneath the primordial moon, kissed by the Gods of the Air, Sun, and Earth. She is lovely. She is lethal. Treat her well, and she will be as a favored lover. But fail to revere her power, and she will consume all who cross her paths.

Calypso is but a mirage, an image of a beautiful woman with the heart of a stone. She knows no love save for that of her children, who live within the bosom of her briny depths. Be wary, man, not to fall slave to her hypnotic spell, for with one kiss, your doom will be sealed...

~Poem writ by Sir Alexander III, third Knight of Venetia circa Kingdom, 1082

A fable penned by the hands of a foolish man. Calypso is ancient and a creature most terrifying to behold. But I know who she really is, and now, too, so will you. The truths of the queens of our stories I will share with you, dear reader, for many of the dark queens of Kingdom have been treated ill—a transgression I seek to rectify now.

Who am I, you might wonder?

Truth is, you already know me. But I wish my privacy to remain intact. Wonder and guess all you like, but at the end of the day, all I seek to do is show the world the true stories of the queens they already thought they knew.

And so now this tale begins as many others do.

Once upon a time...

~ Anonymous, one of the 13 keepers of the ***Tales.***

Chapter 1

Calypso

I stirred from my slumber the moment the first body floated toward me.

Cocking my head, I stared at the face, lined and weathered by years spent under the sun. The woman was slight, appearing almost childlike with her small, slender legs and arms. Silvery hair undulated like a forest of sea kelp behind her.

Even in death she wore a serene smile, the look of a soul who'd lived life well and on her own terms.

I trailed a finger along the cold flesh of her face, her coloration nothing more than shades of pearlescent blue and white. I knew immediately what she was.

The spirit of the dead.

A life thread cut short by the weighted shears of the three Fates.

What I didn't know was why she was here. No sooner had I thought it than another body appeared, and another, and another, each carried on a current, looking like a macabre trail as far as my eye could see.

The blue shades were a blight on the golden waters of my home.

My hippocampus, Linx, lifted her head, whinnying at me softly, immediately sensing my discord.

The creature and I had been born together under the same blood-red moon eons ago, she with the head of a horse and the body of a sea dragon and I bearing the image of a woman but both of us born of the same father.

"Linx." I held out my hand to her. "I don't like this."

Unfurling herself like a large polar cat, she stood twice as tall as me. Her coat was a magnificent mother of pearl, while her tail gleamed turquoise with threads of gold bisecting each scale.

Her teeth were large, capable of tearing a man in half, and her eyes glowed a deep bloody red. She was fury and wonder, and I adored her.

Tossing her head, she caused the waters around us to swirl and thrash angrily.

"I'm not angry, my love. Calm yourself."

I set a hand to her velvety nose. She took several deep breaths, instantly quieting herself and the waves.

Closing my eyes, I "felt," becoming once more who I really was: the very beating, living essence of liquid life. Water was in everything. There was no place in all the stars closed off to me. I existed in all things, and all things existed in me.

I smiled as above me, otters played, sighed as lovers sank into my cool depths, loving one another for the first time, heart quickening as my children grew and learned and lived.

But as I stretched my senses, I felt the disturbance reach farther than the Under, farther even than the hallowed black depths of the deepest below, all the way to the Underworld itself.

Opening my eyes, I turned to Linx. I could still sense her discord. Her nostrils flared rapidly as she sniffed the fresh, clean scent of salt and sea flowers now mingled with a slight trace of sweet almond odor, a smell typically associated with the freshly dead.

The Gates are sealed.

Linx's thoughts swirled through my head.

"You know this?"

Where I could feel any disturbance, Linx was more attuned to scent. She could form an image from smell alone just like a predatory fish could, only more keenly and sharply than any other creature in creation.

The scent of golden dew is absent.

I frowned. "Are you sure?"

"Golden dew" was how Linx referred to Persephone, Goddess of the Spring, and Hades'...something.

The tales were never quite clear on those two.

"Zeus," I muttered. The absolute last place in hell I wanted to be was literally in Hell. The day I was born, I quit the pantheon.

I hated the pettiness of the gods and goddesses, the muckraking, and the constant schemes for power. It was why I'd parked my big, fat, watery ass in Kingdom and stayed put.

Pinching my brows, I shook my head. "Well, I'm not going back there. Hades can just handle this himself."

Linx frowned, which was actually a grotesque movement of upper and lower lips pulling back to expose the shearing strength of blunt, wide teeth. I lifted a brow.

"You don't scare me, horse face."

Anybody else, and Linx probably would have eaten them for such an insult.

The bodies will only continue to circle our waters.

Which wouldn't normally be a problem; the sharks could handle a few hundred thousand bodies in a day with a little gentle persuasion and some blood in the water. But already I could feel my snaggle-toothed babies going crazy with fury. The bodies felt and smelled very real, but they were little more than ghosts in the water.

There was only one being in all creation that could clean this mess up before it got further out of hand.

"Why has that damn Persephone not opened the bloody gates already!" I stomped my foot, causing the tectonic plates beneath to shift and grumble furiously.

This time, Linx was the one lifting a shaggy brow at me.

You've spent far too much time with your son's mate. You're beginning to sound like her.

Linx was of course referring to the highly entertaining Nimue. I merely shrugged a shoulder.

"She does not know it is really me. Our anonymity is quite safe, I can assure you, sister." I smiled sweetly.

You're stalling, woman. You know we must go to him. Now...

Linx turned, offering me her back. It was sweet of her to offer. But I knew how much she dreaded leaving these waters. Hippocampus were creatures of habit, almost to an extreme degree. They very rarely went farther than a twenty-mile radius in any one direction for the entirety of their lives—which in her case, was eternal.

She was my best and truest friend. I hated to leave her, but...

"I'll go alone."

I tried not to sound as grumpy as I felt, but I failed spectacularly.

Linx thinned her lips.

"I'm fine, really. But if I don't come back in three days, Hades did it, and you should drown him."

Snuffling softly, Linx floated gently back to the ground, curled her tail tight around herself, nodded, and promptly fell back to sleep.

In seconds, the water churned with the bubbles of her snoring.

"So heartwarming to know how well I am loved," I muttered sarcastically beneath my breath.

Then, slipping once more back into the form most comfortable to me, I drifted through the currents as swiftly as thought.

My waterways moved like a giant network of roads, with my domicile in Kingdom being its central hub. In mere seconds, I'd slipped out of the waters of Seren and into the River Styx.

The disparity in landscapes between the two couldn't have been more shocking. Where Kingdom was full of light and sunshine, the waters sparkled like cut crystal, and sea life abounded, in Styx there was nothing but the acrid stench of sulfur, rocks that glistened with molten veins of lava, and chimney stacks that belched black, noxious funnels of water.

Even the skies above were dark and foreboding; the only light came from pits of literal flame interspersed at odd intervals throughout the otherwise dead and barren land of the Underworld.

I curled my nose, wanting nothing more than to turn around and go back home.

"Who disturbs my waters?" a deep and scratchy voice that sounded like dead leaves dancing upon asphalt boomed.

Taking a form that I could speak in, I rose from the river as little more than a pillar of shimmering water and smirked at Charon. The Riverman, as I liked to call him (because calling him a walking skeleton with holes for eyes and bones for hands wasn't the most polite thing in the world to do), dipped his head swiftly.

"Calypso," the angry burr he'd had just moments ago vanished beneath shock.

So okay, maybe I'd become a bit of a recluse lately. Like, say, the past eternity or so.

"What are you doing here?" he asked quickly as he sank his paddle back into the waters, slowly ferrying the dead from the land of the living to the land of...well, the dead, of course.

I pursed my lip. "Char, baby, I can call you Char, right?"

"Well, I—"

I waved a hand, shushing him instantly. "I'm here to see Hades. He does still live here, right?"

The water frothed beneath my feet.

If it was possible for a skeleton to gulp, I was pretty sure he'd just done it.

"Of...of course, goddess."

Giving him a tight smile, I swished at my imaginary skirts and sauntered by, head held high.

"Moron," I grumped when he was safely out of hearing distance.

Not that I didn't like Skeletor, but...okay, I didn't like Skeletor. I didn't like being here. I didn't like these kind of dead, the ones that just floated by and didn't blink, didn't twitch, didn't even say boo. It made me twitchy and grumpy.

So sue me.

I wanted desperately to sink back into the water, but it was teeming with ghost zombies, piles and piles of them. So I had to make do with stepping from one to the next, all the while pretending in my head I was walking on a swinging bridge and not cold, squishy chest parts.

I'd been practicing the past few years, perfecting what it meant to be "human": how to laugh properly, act properly.

For too long I'd been nothing but the unseen presence of the deep, a heartbeat without form.

Thanks to Sircco's crazy but wonderful bride, I'd learned the language of the people, and prided myself now on being able to interact well with others. Like, for instance, I had learned that when someone stole from me, the answer wasn't always to drown them.

Maybe sometimes they were just hungry and needed food desperately. In those cases, a pardon was in order. Of course, with the threat of cutting off one's balls should they ever try it again.

Or one time, I'd even managed to restrain my violent temper when a pack of bawdy sailors had kidnapped one of my sea maidens, attempting to rape her. Instead of following my first inclination of sinking their ship, opening up a fissure in the earth so that lava spewed up from its guts and boiled them alive, I instead chopped off their balls, boiled them in onion water, and fed them to Bruce, my pet great white.

I was rather proud of myself for that level of restraint. They may no longer be able to sire bastards, but at least they were alive. Win-win-win, so far as I was concerned.

Yes, I was much better at handling my anger now.

Which was why I was going to march in there, tell Hades to open the damn gates (nicely, of course), and then get back home ASAP (another fun little word I'd learned from Nim).

I was just about within spitting distance of the Bony Gates—a very large and menacing gate built of nothing but knuckles and long bones that gleamed a creamy white color—when something caused me to pause.

The Underworld was divided into two regions. On the left was Tartarus: black, leeched of any color save for the red glow of flame, where the screams of the damned were an eternal and lonely wail. And to the right were the Elysian Fields, which were as lovely as the name sounded.

I wasn't much into land, but if I had to be stuck in any one place for long, I'd choose here. It was a land teeming with wildflowers, with breezes that smelled of every conceivable scent of rose imaginable, where no one aged, because no matter how old you were when you died, you returned to this place hale and whole and more beautiful than you'd been even in life.

Just a sip of the water running through this place could sustain you for a thousand years.

Even now two lovers were cavorting nearby.

My heart raced as a beautiful man with a sharply square jaw and shaggy dark hair lifted a hand toward a woman's hair that seemed spun from the sun itself. They were both nude and gazing at one another with such fierce longing that it brought heat to my cheeks.

I nibbled on my bottom lip, telling myself I should look away and give them some semblance of privacy.

"Oh, hell," I mumbled, not like they'd care anyway.

My eyes widened when he dropped to his knees. There was no wooing, no sweet words whispered; he took her in his mouth.

Down there.

Not that I was shy or anything. I mean, I'd had a gaggle of children. I understood the mechanics of sex. I saw the animals doing it all the time.

And felt the waves rock when my son and his bride "cavorted."

I felt the life of that act move through my bones like ambrosia, and I couldn't help but lean forward on my toes a little when she gasped, clutching the Bony Gates with white-knuckled fingers.

The body I stood on dipped beneath me as I shifted again.

"Oh, Zeus." I clutched at my chest, imagining it was that lovely man's fingers on my naked body, caressing me, fondling me...touching me down there, with his tongue.

As many children as I'd had, I'd never actually lain with a man. Not once.

Odd thing was, once upon a time, I didn't used to care about that. Even prided myself on that fact. Like Artemis and Athena, I'd found men *lacking*.

But now I couldn't help but wonder whether there was something to this "sexing" thing.

I wet my lips when the woman finally flung her head back and screamed with such rapture that the buds at her feet bloomed brightly.

The man came up for a kiss, and in less than no time, they were off and scampering away like two currently satisfied but still horny bunnies.

As I blinked back to reality, it took me a minute to realize the body I stood on was starting to drift away from where I wished to go.

Glancing around quickly just to make sure no one caught me gawking like a horny bunny myself, I shook off the strange feelings and hopscotched my way across the bodies until finally my feet touched land.

Clearing my throat, I glanced down at myself. Normally I walked with a watery form, but for some reason, today I was feeling "funky."

I frowned, not quite sure I was using the right word here, but no matter. Squaring my shoulders, I tweaked my form just slightly, making myself more fleshy, less watery.

But then I felt rather dull, so I added just a touch of mother of pearl to my skin so that as I walked, there was a sheen. I saw Nimue do it once. She'd found some sort of lotion and had whispered in my ear that when she'd applied it the night before, Sircco had nearly lost his mind with need.

Not that anyone around here would appreciate my efforts.

Still...

In short order, I'd turned my sea-kelp hair into actual maiden hair that ended at my ass. It was now a stunning shade of soft sea-foam green and curled attractively around nubile breasts.

Nimue said men preferred their women nude.

"When in Roman," I whispered, not really quite sure what exactly that meant, but Nimue said it all the time. Especially when she was trying out new things.

Or maybe she said something else? I couldn't quite recall.

"Bloody hell," I mumbled, more nervous than I had a right to be. Gripping my stomach, I studied the gates. Why was Cerberus not around?

The mangy, three-headed demon dog was always guarding the gates. Not only was Persephone missing, now too was the fleabag.

Pursing my lips, both annoyed and irritated, I figured there was nothing to do other than to push the massive gates open myself.

They opened with nary a squeak.

Immediately the backlog of bodies began to push through, being carted off to their proper places of eternal rest.

Huffing, I followed the Elysian trail toward Hades' home.

A gentle breeze perfumed my bare flesh. The sky was blue. White birds dipped and dived through the air. Bees buzzed. It was all very nauseatingly perfect.

For a God of Death *he sure is annoyingly cheerful*, I thought.

And where was that damn god, anyway? Why was I seeing no servants rush up to meet me? Hades had always struck me as the pompous sort, theatrical in all he did.

I mean, one look around this ridiculous place—

"Oh, crab apples!" I gasped with delight, veering off the trail to pluck up a juicy red apple in the shape of a crab off a tree. They were my absolute favorites and quite difficult to obtain twenty leagues under the sea.

Taking an enormous bite, I groaned at the salty sweetness of crab-scented apple flesh.

In moments, I spied the grand mansion of the Under Lord himself. The stones that'd built it were as black and foreboding as his very soul. The architecture was Gothic, with massive gargoyles perched on top, claws flared wide as though ready to eviscerate you.

I smiled, quite liking the look of it already.

But still, there were no souls about.

Not even the dead ones. Elysia was devoid of all human life at the moment.

I'd be offended, but then I saw a strip of vivid red splashed along the dirt. When I noticed that, I immediately noticed a rather large strip of grass and dirt blackened by soot and still smoldering as though from a recently banked flame.

Tossing the apple core to the ground, I sniffed the air, scenting a peculiar odor. Tangy. Sweet. And dangerously venomous. Seren cone snail.

I frowned. Seren cone snails were bloodthirsty, devilish little creatures. Known for their paralyzing toxins, they could floor a sea maiden with one prick of their harpoons, knocking her out for days, sometimes even weeks, depending on the dosage administered.

They were also deep-sea-dwelling creatures and should definitely not have been here.

Lightning flashed, and the heavens suddenly quaked.

Glancing to the sky, I shook my head and groaned.

"You deny that you killed her!" Zeus's voice was like thunder, rocking through the grounds.

More curious now than ever, I shook off my fleshy form like a dog shaking rain from its coat and called to the water in the sky, hiding within a droplet of it, seeking out quickly why the king of gods had deigned to show his face in Hell.

What I spied was more than I'd expected. Not only was Zeus here, but there was a crowd of gods. A pantheon of them, in fact. And at the very center was a giant of a man shackled in iron and yet holding his head high as he glared holy fury at the lot of them.

Chapter 2

Hades

Fury tore me up from the inside.

Persephone was missing. Cerberus was presumed dead. And the entire horde of gods believed I'd done it.

Themis stood before me, carrying a set of golden scales in her hand, with a white cloth tied around her eyes. Completely blind, she was also the Goddess of Justice.

She was cold, unmoving, and little more than a statue until the moment she handed down judgment.

I growled, looking at a glowering Demeter.

She stood before me, a regal beauty dressed in silks stained the colors of wheat, earth, and grass. Her nut-brown hair was coiled tightly about her oval face. She was not classically beautiful, but there was a sturdy handsomeness about her that had always attracted me.

Of all the gods on Olympus, I'd often thought her the most levelheaded of the bunch.

Until her daughter had turned up missing.

Rich brown eyes turned aside.

Clenching my jaw, I glanced elsewhere. My last hope had been a sign of goodwill from her.

Sneering, I stared down my arrogant brothers Zeus and Poseidon.

"It is not enough that you've cast me into this festering Hell; now you threaten torture! Do it, then. Do what you've always wanted to do anyway, *brothers*."

Seeing as how a god could not be killed, the Olympians had almost created a sport of inventive ways to torture, be it being racked and laid out for the vultures to pick at my eyeballs for the next hundred years or being shut in a box and tossed into the ocean to continually drown and awaken over and over and over again.

The skies above suddenly opened with rain.

Rain in the Underworld never happened.

I glanced at Zeus and then at Poseidon (as the God of the Seas); he had the ability to control rain, too. But they both looked as puzzled as I felt.

Then Poseidon sneered, "Consort, show yourself."

Consort?

That could only mean one thing. But Calypso never left the safety of her waters.

I sucked in a shocked breath when the droplets formed into the image of a woman more lovely than even the Goddess of Love herself. She sparkled like dew in the soft morning sun.

Hair of the softest green cascaded long and thick in waves down her back and front. She wore no clothes. And each time she shifted, I caught just a glimmer of tight, firm, rounded flesh.

As if unaware of the spectacle she'd made of herself, Calypso planted her hands on her hips and cocked her head, causing a tiny array of golden seahorses to glimmer like copper pennies in her hair.

And her eyes, when she turned them on me, burned like hottest flame.

"Your ghosts are fouling my waters, Dead Boy."

Everyone gasped.

But not I. I was too devoid of thought to even think of uttering a sound. In all the years I'd known Calypso, two things were constant. One, she never wandered far from her home, preferring instead to live life as a water elemental rather than take on fleshy form. And two, she never spoke.

Not to those above land.

I couldn't seem to pull my eyes away from the sheer beauty of a body I'd never quite imagined she'd possessed.

Poseidon was the first to shake the stupor off. "What are you doing here, woman?"

A long time ago, the two had been engaged.

A long, long time ago.

Around the dawn of time, to be precise.

Poseidon had called her a bitch with a heart of ice, and she'd caused a worldwide flood in return. Needless to say, the two didn't get on.

Aphrodite curled her lip. Practically six foot, with a body built for sin, blond hair that fell past her knees, blue eyes that could rival the color of a cloudless sky, and a face that'd caused many a man to beg for death at the chance of having just one taste of her lips, she gazed calculatingly at a very naked sea goddess.

Suddenly the already sheer gown she wore turned completely translucent, and a wave of her power bowled through men and women alike. She hardly cared who worshipped her so long as they worshipped her.

I panted beneath the strain of a now raging erection, as did most of the others around me.

Even Artemis's—the Virgin Huntress's—eyes had gone wide, and her pupils dilated.

Calypso crossed her arms, pushing her already voluptuous mounds upward, prominently displaying them, and inclined her head as though in acknowledgement of Aphrodite's prowess.

The Goddess of Love was a passionate, sometimes volatile woman and was known to have bouts of intense jealousy and rage when she felt in the slightest bit threatened by another.

It was a shock to see her lips twitch with what seemed more like amusement than disdain.

Turning a mercurial gaze on me, Calypso lifted a brow and tapped her foot.

"Well," she snapped, "have you nothing to say to me?"

"Calypso, what is the meaning of this interruption?" Zeus shook himself as if coming awake after a numbed stupor, his grizzly bear–sized form intimidating to all but the main pantheon of gods.

As far as the gods went, Calypso wasn't one of us, and that was mostly due to her hermit nature, even though her powers were equally as formidable—some even whispered superior. But instead of cowering in Zeus's presence, she leveled her chin.

Where she'd been bristly just a moment before, now she seemed contemplative as her intelligent gaze quickly took us all in. Her moods were said to shift as quickly as the turning of the tides.

"Why is Death in chains?" she asked calmly but with a tone that brooked nothing less than immediate answers.

I couldn't help but smirk when Zeus's eyes bulged and his lips tightened to a razor's edge.

Lightning cut jaggedly through the sky.

"Strike at me, and I'll flood your hairy ass." Heavy drops of rain punctuated her statement.

Her words were measured, even, without the slightest pause for dramatic effect, which made the threat all the more believable.

Zeus was Zeus, but even he knew not to further anger a crazy woman.

"They believe I've committed treason." I finally spoke to her, my cadence as calm as hers had been.

Turning on her heel so that she faced me head on, she lifted a brow. A gentle breeze stirred the strands of hair hanging over her breasts, revealing tantalizing glimpses of shell-pink nipples. The weight of her stare felt heavy, almost oppressive. Had I been a mortal, I'd be dead now.

"And did you?"

Themis cleared her throat, looking directly in Calypso's direction. "He is being tried now, Goddess of the Sea."

Calypso's laughter reminded me of the roar of waves slapping against wet sand.

"I know your methodology of justice, blindy. I am not amused."

I couldn't hide my grin.

I'd always thought of the seas as being deep but placid—impenetrable and at times terrifying, but also awe inspiring. I'd mistakenly attributed those traits to Calypso as well, and I could not have been more wrong. Oh, she was awe inspiring, but there was nothing placid about this woman.

She had the tongue of a shrew and a body built to inspire odes.

"You have no purpose being here," Hera snapped, her cow eyes flashing furiously as she took a threatening step in Calypso's direction.

The raindrops that'd been little more than an annoyance suddenly increased in strength.

It was Zeus who stopped Hera, placing a restraining hand against her chest. "Don't," he warned.

Poseidon's dark-blue hair began to coil and writhe like charmed sea snakes about his head.

Calypso rolled her eyes. "Oh please, fish butt. We've danced this tango before."

"Enough!" Zeus held up his hands as the skies cracked. "The worlds cannot survive another one of your spats. Put your pricks away, if you please." He stared at both Poseidon and Calypso.

"He started it," Calypso murmured, curling her nose in utter disgust and defiance.

Poseidon shook himself, causing a trail of hermit crabs to drop from his hair to the grassy floor and scuttle off in a mad bid to hide.

Aphrodite laughed as though wonderfully delighted by the sudden turn the day's events had taken.

But it was Demeter's gentle presence that calmed our moods.

"I only wish to learn of my daughter's fate," she whispered. "Tell us where she's at, Hades. Where did you hide her body?"

Calypso

Hide the body?

Did they think Persephone dead?

Looking at Hades, I could see that was what they thought exactly. His jaw was clenched tight, making the muscle in his cheek jump and snap. Fury vibrated off his taut, firm shoulders.

I'd come to find out why the dork had let bodies pile up in my demesne, but now I found myself with an entirely different reason to stay.

When had Hades gotten to be so hawt?

That was the way Nim had said it once. That Sircco was *hawwwt*. She'd fanned herself while saying it, which had led me to believe that was an entirely different level of handsome. It was something beyond mere aesthetics, more like..."You are both handsome, and I wish to slather you in oils and sex you up."

Or at least that's how I'd understood it.

I very much wanted to slather Hades' body in oil and have my wicked, wicked way with him.

I would start with his thighs maybe. Dig my claws into them, make him moan and writhe and beg and then hop on his stiffy and bounce my way up and down to satisfaction. I'd seen a sailor and his bride doing that through a porthole once, and it'd looked erotically glorious.

But my daydreams were being continuously interrupted by the shouting going on around me.

There was more blathering going on. Hephaestus—the little midget of a man with a wicked mustache and a shocking flame of orange hair—was shaking his fist at Apollo.

Beautiful Apollo with his golden smile and equally radiant head of hair was smirking down at the little man with the pompous arrogance of a prick. It was rumored Apollo preferred men to women. A shame, too; I might have enjoyed riding him.

Then again, there was a dark attraction to the broody, mesmerizing Hades that beckoned me in a way Apollo's sunny glories could not.

Talk of bloodstained earth, Cerberus being gone...blah blah blah. I found myself annoyed by the lot of them all over again.

The blowhards were so bloody self-absorbed that they'd probably never notice if I just up and left now.

The gates were open now, the bodies polluting my waters no more. Technically I could leave and none would care.

I looked back at Hades and realized that somehow I'd taken two steps closer to his side. I sniffed as his scent seemed to draw around me—patchouli and wood smoke.

It was oddly...interesting.

I sniffed again.

From the corner of my eye, I caught Dite staring at me thoughtfully. I glanced up.

"What?" I asked.

She approached me, her big, beautiful eyes blinking back at me. "You smell of lust, Sea. I find that rather intriguing. Are you not a virgin goddess?"

I snorted. "If I smell of lust, can you blame me? Your stench washes through this place."

A long red fingernail tapped upon her slightly pointy chin. "No, that's not it. I recognize my own scent. This is different. And may I say, you look different, too. Last time I saw you, you were far more cool and reserved."

There'd been a time in my not-too-distant past when I'd remained private and aloof, keeping no company other than Linx's. I'd been content to take care of the children of Seren and wonder about nothing more.

But Nimue was a breath of fresh air, one I'd never even realized I'd needed.

I shrugged. "Times change."

Straight white teeth gleamed. "You speak differently, too. Far more modern."

I crossed my arms. "What is your point, wench?"

The tinkling sound of Dite's laughter broke me out in a wash of goose flesh. No one around us seemed to notice or care that we carried on a conversation all our own.

"My point is, I rather like it." She waggled her brows. "I've grown tired of this lot, but being around you, my love, is like drinking the sweet dew of ambrosia. I think we should be friends."

I frowned. "I think I should drown you."

"See!" Aphrodite snuffled with laughter. The sound was entirely unladylike, and yet with her being the Goddess of Love and all, the sound was positively charming. "You are wonderful. I do not need to worry about you smiling in my face and shoving a dagger in my back."

The thought did not compute. "If I was going to shove a dagger into you, I'd do it while you looked on."

I was confused that she'd believe otherwise; stabbing one in the back was bad form. Bad form indeed.

Wrapping an arm around my shoulders, she squeezed me gently. "How have I gone my whole life without knowing you, dear one?"

"Because I find you all to be beastly bores."

Amusement continued to sparkle through her lovely eyes. She confused me.

"I agree. Truth be told," she leaned in to whisper hotly in my ear, "I only came here today because Hephy made me."

By some quirk of fate, the enchanting creature before me had fallen madly in love with the deformed little imp Hephaestus. Theirs was an odd match, but it was rumored to be a healthy one.

So far as Olympian matches went, that was.

"What are they doing to Hades?" When I said his name, I looked back at him and again experienced a wonderfully delicious sensation of heat whipping like lava through my veins.

He had a face that would make a master sculptor weep. Classically handsome, with dark, swarthy features. Deep, impenetrable eyes. Yes, I wanted him as my first sex partner.

"Whew," Dite lifted her hand off me and shook her fingers. "You're positively brimming with raw lust. So you want to have Count Dracula's babies, do you?"

"Count Dracula? No, I do not know of whom you speak. Nor do I wish more children. I have plenty. I just want to screw Hades' liver out."

Dite blinked. "I believe the expression is 'screw his brains out.'"

"Whatever." I shrugged. Nimue often laughed at my inability to form proper phrases. "I want him."

"What would you be willing to do to get him?"

"Make him my sex slave?" The thought had honestly never occurred to me. But now that it did, there was some merit to it. I could already imagine that big, brawny body strapped to my bed, naked and pleading for mercy.

I grinned.

"Not a slave, dear. You cannot enslave any of us."

"Oh, I could enslave him. Without my permission to breathe below, he'd drown. He would be required to do my bidding in all things."

"Such a deviant mind, Sea. I love it!" Dite clapped her hands prettily.

Everything about her was pretty. I might have been nauseated were it not for the fact that she currently amused me.

Themis held up her scales of justice.

Aphrodite leaned in. “They are about to pass judgment, and once it is passed, his fate is sealed. Which means you have less than a minute to decide if sexing up Hades is worth it.”

“What can I do?”

“All here believe Hades has orchestrated a plot to have Persephone removed from his Underworld. Offer to take him as your prisoner instead.”

Anyone who knew the two of them wouldn’t have a hard time believing that to be true. Persephone was the apple of her mother’s eye and a giant douche bag. She was spoiled, rotten, and self-centered.

Hades was also vile, loathsome, and fiercely dangerous.

My heart sped.

I stepped forward just as Themis opened her mouth.

“Excuse me, ladies and gents,” I curtsied quickly, flashing my most winsome and innocent smile. “I think we got off on the wrong fin here.”

“Calypso,” Zeus said through gritted teeth, “step aside before I make you step aside.”

My smile vanished. But it was the quick shake of Dite’s head that held my tongue. Swallowing my anger, I pinched out another smile, this one not quite as believable as the last one.

“What I’m trying to say here is, I want him.” I pointed at Hades, who now had his head bowed and seemed to be glaring furiously at the ground.

“Want him?” Poseidon snapped. “You are mine.”

“Oh, piss off, fish fart.”

Zeus held up his hand. “Olympus save me,” he groaned. “Calypso, the evidence is clear. Hades has either killed Persephone or knows the fate that has befallen her. Either way, he must be made to pay. And unless you have new evidence to present—”

I smiled sweetly. “Well actually, thunder butt, I do.”

He gnashed his teeth, and Aphrodite looked like she was about to come unglued from suppressed laughter.

Themis's scales tipped sharply downward. "She speaks truth."

Hera rubbed the bridge of her nose furiously. As Queen of the Pantheon, she had equal rights to demand answers in this trial. "Then tell us, Calypso, for all our sakes."

Walking over to Hades, I once again was cocooned in the warmth of his scent. Placing a hand on his shoulder until he looked into my eyes, I asked him, "Oh, God of Darkness, tell me, when was the last time you left this hellhole?"

"I've not left in thirty-seven years and fifty-six days."

The scales leveled out.

"Truth," Themis decreed.

Turning to the crowd, I held out my arms, striking a dramatic pose. If there was anything in this world more dramatic than the waters of the deep, I did not know it.

"So you see, it was not him."

"That literally tells us nothing." Zeus shook his head.

I rolled my eyes. "Poseidon, you ignorant fool, tell them what you smelled back in the blood-soaked field."

His eyes widened, and as I'd suspected, I knew he'd withheld one very important, key bit of evidence from the bloodthirsty mob.

Zeus twirled on his brother, his white beard beginning to darken and fluff up like a thundercloud. "What did you smell, *brother*?"

Behind me, I sensed rather than saw Hades' head snap up.

"Just because I smelled it doesn't mean that Hades wasn't involved in some way. We all know the history of loathing that exists between the two."

"What the hell did you smell!" Zeus roared. A flash of lightning struck at Poseidon's heel, making him jerk away.

"If you weren't all so quick to make snap judgments—" I said and then was rudely interrupted.

"You're one to talk," a deep male voice said. My coral was on Apollo.

I smiled; he'd be getting a nasty surprise when he got home later to discover his once-immaculate mansion now dripping with seawater and kelp.

Pressing on, I ignored his little jab. For now. "—then you'd know that the air reeked of Seren cone snail. A nasty little creature with a most venomous touch. That, oh," I tapped a finger to my chin, "lives in the deepest parts of my waters and cannot survive more than fifteen minutes in the Above before dying. Poor dear. To be frank, there are so few of us here who could possibly get our hands on one that I'd be more apt to lay the blame on fish breath first."

"You devilish hag!" Poseidon roared, and rain fell in thick sheets around us all.

But I remained toasty and dry, tossing up a deflective shield over not only myself but also Dite (since I rather liked her after all) and Hades because he was hawt and I wished to bang the liver out of him.

Everyone began yelling then, snarling at Poseidon to turn off the waterworks. I merely stuck out my tongue at him.

Themis's scales leveled out. "All true. Judgment must now be delayed until I can study the new evidence that has come to light."

Demeter lifted a hand. "Until Persephone is discovered, I cannot allow Hades to remain here. If her body is buried here, he'll try to—"

"You have no right!" Hades finally spoke up for himself. "I've told you often enough what your daughter has done. Her wildness has led her here. This is not on me!"

"And yet her soul screams out to me!" Demeter snapped, her eyes brimming over with tears.

I did feel a small thread of sympathy; after all, I was a mother myself. Should any of my precious babies be lost to me thus, I'd lose my poop. Or was that shit?

Probably shit.

Poop sounded so silly.

I sighed. "I want him. I'll take him. Considering he cannot leave my waters unless I grant it, he will be perfectly tortured until you can discover where Persephone has gone."

"Tortured?" Dite frowned, obviously thinking I'd misspoken again, but this time I hadn't.

I did mean to torture him. In every conceivable way. I'd make him scream my name to the very heavens. My thighs tingled at the thought.

"Calypso," Poseidon drawled, no doubt ready to go all caveman on me again and claim me as his own.

We hated each other, and yet he hated to lose what was "his" more.

"Oh, shut your trap and go mate another porpoise."

Themis shook her head. "I will now pass judgment."

She had to mostly scream to be heard above the hullaballoo. "Calypso, Goddess of the Sea, your request has been granted. You shall keep Hades within your Kingdom for the next fortnight. He cannot be allowed into the Above for any reason while we follow the evidentiary trail toward the true culprit. Should he escape, he will be lashed a thousand times by Athena's whip, chained to a rock, and have his eyes picked on by vultures for the next thousand years."

"Oh, is that all?" Hades growled.

My lips twitched. He was funny.

"Hades, should all signs still point to you, however, you will suffer the fate laid out after the two weeks are up. I hope these terms are sufficient for all."

It wasn't a question, but I answered anyway.

"Not really."

"Good," Zeus boomed. "Then take him and go."

Chapter 3

Calypso

Hades wasn't particularly keen on my method of transportation. I'd already had to knock a watery fist into his thick skull a time or twenty to get him to stop screaming at me as we sank beneath the waves.

"If you stop screaming, you'll stop swallowing so much damned water," I said sweetly, plastering on a tight smile.

He could breathe. Sort of.

I hadn't given him the kiss of life yet, but it was kind of fun to have him completely at my mercy and clinging to my body like a man drowning.

He pinned me with a cold, obsidian glare, clamping his full, kissable lips shut and snarling hate at me. Seriously. I saw the hate just bubbling off his shoulders like pools of heated lava.

"You can breathe, you know."

He shoved his face to within an inch of my own, his nostrils flaring like Linx's sometimes would when she was really angry. Aw, he was so cute.

"Only when I'm clamped onto your side like a foul leech. Kiss me and allow me to retain at least a small measure of dignity here, Calypso."

My heart beat faster than a hoodoo priestess banging on her drums.

"You only needed to ask, Dead Boy."

The waters around us were a black so deep it seemed bottomless, but my body glowed like a raft of mating kreels. I glimmered every shade of blue and knew I looked beautiful.

Hades might dislike me right now, but he was enraptured by me. I could see it in his eyes. Many a man had lost his heart to the Sea. He'd not be the first. But the Sea had never lost her heart to any man.

Still, when I dug my nails into the curve of his ass and yanked him to me, it was I who trembled.

I'd seen sex. Too many times to count. Seen the courtship before and after. I knew what I was doing. But I'd never technically done it before.

Still, how hard could it be? Insert tab into slot, grunt, writhe, moan, boom...sex. Easy.

I bet it didn't even feel all that great.

Opening my mouth, I called to the life inside me, the sweet nectar of air that I would gift upon him with one press of my lips to his.

I warned all creatures away from me. I wanted nothing and no one to hinder my first-ever, honest-to-Kingdom kiss.

"Open your mouth," I commanded him.

Smart man that he was, he didn't argue.

He opened, and then the tip of his tongue swiped along his upper lip, and I couldn't stop myself anymore. With a groan, I slammed my mouth to his. Just this touch was sufficient to let him breathe. I felt his chest inflate as my air became his. I knew he could move unhindered now, but he was mine. At least for the next two weeks.

So I altered the kiss just slightly. And then I stopped thinking about altered kisses when his tongue swiped along the inside seam of my lips. Greedy, I sucked him in, twining my tongue through his.

He tasted of power, divine, magnificent, colossal power. Every inch of my body felt electrified by his deadly touch.

Hades was the keeper of the dead. Be you a mortal, to touch him would mean to seal your doom. To taste of his flesh would feel like bathing in the pits of Tartarus for an eternity.

But for me...ye gods.

The Seren seas churned. Waves rocked upon the shores. My children crawled from out of their caves, their homes, aware of the primal magick just released upon them.

I moved my hands from his ass to the rock-hard planes of his back and up to the nape of his neck. Nimue said that if you clawed at a man's head just lightly, with a tiny little scrape, they'd come undone.

I scraped, and Hades shuddered.

His hard fingers dug into my shoulders, the grip firm and punishing. And it was glorious.

I purred into the back of my throat when I finally pulled away, licking my lips like a very contented kittycat.

Hades looked supremely pleased with himself. His dark hair was a mussed mess around his broad forehead.

"I could leave you now, Sea. Disappear through these waters and never return," he mocked.

I cocked my head, the glow of my body even brighter in intensity than before. There wasn't an inch of me that didn't tingle. I laughed.

"Why, because I've kissed life into your lungs? Do you truly believe me fool enough to give you all of me? There is none that can tame the Sea. Remember that, my precious Reaper."

He took a deep breath. "I am a god, Calypso. You cannot own me."

"Who said I wanted to own you? I just want your body. Your..." I glanced down at his very obviously bulging package. "...prick. The kiss I granted you may not consider much of a gift in time, soon-to-be lover."

Narrowing his eyes, he shook his head. "What have you done to me?"

I shrugged, trailing a finger down the razor-sharp plane of his left cheek. "I've only made you dizzy with dependency for me.

For the next two weeks, you are my slave. So suck it up, Bubble Butt."

That had sounded wrong. *Hm.*

Frowning, he glanced over his shoulder at his delectable rear. "Are you sure you meant to say—"

Waving his words away, I grabbed his hand and yanked him down into the abyss with me. Linx was really not going to like my surprise. But just this once, I wasn't sure I cared.

He was mine; she could run off and get her own toy if she wanted too.

My children, aware that they were no longer required to keep their distance from us, soon squeezed in on us from all sides.

Goblin sharks, their razor teeth gleaming as their mouths hung open like cute little panting puppies, stared curiously at me and hungrily at Hades.

"Go away, my darlings," I cooed.

"Darlings," Hades shuddered, "They look more like globs of steaming dung with beady eyes."

I gave him a droll look. "Say one more word against them and I'll let them have you for a light snack later."

Moray and electric eels slithered between our bodies, pressing their flattened tails to my cheeks in greeting.

Fish of every color of the rainbow peeked at us curiously, scuttling off when a giant, fanged wolf shark suddenly made its appearance and snapped up a tiny lamprey eel on its way back down into the abyss.

Hades clenched his jaw.

"Do not tell me my children frighten you, God of Death," I smirked.

His eyes were full of mystery as they turned toward me. I wished I knew what he was thinking.

"What are you thinking?" I asked, too impatient to play guessing games.

He spread his arms. "You act as though you care."

I might have been offended by his words, but his tone seemed more thoughtful than accusatory. So instead I shrugged.

"I do care. I love my children. And they love me, too, don't you, Bruce." I smushed my face against my favorite great white's cartilaged nose. Bruce had been with me as a pup. I'd found him half starved and gored through the side by the rapier edge of a swordfish's snout. I'd nursed him back to health, and now my baby was a fully grown twenty-foot monster with teeth the size of my fist.

Bruce head butted Hades in the center of his back.

"Is he tasting me?" he asked when Bruce's tail snapped his thigh.

"No. What would give you that idea?" I smiled, slapping at Bruce's head when he opened his massive jaws to take a bite out of Hades' delectable ass.

That was my ass, thank you very much.

"Go find your own ass, Bruce. Now go." I flicked my wrist at him.

His look was grumpy, but Bruce always wore a grumpy look. He took an angry swipe at a passing red horned devil octopus, slurping it down in one mighty gulp.

I grimaced. Okay, so maybe he had been tasting Hades.

Moments later, we arrived at my home. It wasn't much, just a simple temple composed entirely of gold, mother of pearl, marble, and coral. The temple stretched a good four hundred feet or so in either direction, with pillars that supported the heavy beams. Every brick of gold gleamed, resplendent in the early-morning wash of light. I was rather fond of my humble abode, if I must say so. As Queen of the Sea, I could have chosen any place in the waters to call home, but this cozy house suited me just fine.

With a thought, I pushed the massive gates open and was immediately greeted by Linx.

But her horsey smile vanished almost instantly the moment her gaze alighted upon my captive.

Why is he here? She demanded. Miniature bolts of lightning sparked off her hooves as she struck the gold-veined marble floor.

I'd still not released Hades' hand. Or maybe he hadn't released mine. I tried to disentangle my fingers and couldn't.

Oh, that was interesting indeed. I grinned.

"I do hear you, you know." His voice was a deep, almost seductive purr, and it made me frown.

"Are you seducing my hippocampus?" I twirled on him, shoving him back with a wall of water.

But Hades was no mere man, and my show of theatrics did not impress him. He brushed off his black coat without answering me and turned to address Linx once more.

"I have nothing but the highest respect for you, dear hippocampus. Your people have always been good to mine. I hope we can remain cordial during my stay here."

"Incarceration," I was quick to correct, noting that his honeyed words had turned my mule of a companion into a puddle of goo.

She now wore a sleepy-eyed, dreamy look. Zeus had once lain with a swan, so it wasn't hard for me to believe there could be some hippocampus-and-Death Boy love a-brewin'.

"My ass," I snipped and slapped my palm to his rock-hard cheek—the one *down there*—and squeezed.

Hades rose on his toes, glowered at me, and then swatted at my hand. "*My* ass. Where is my room, Calypso?"

"Fine." I flicked my fingers, sending him away and locking him in my room.

It was the most comfortable room in the temple anyway. With the biggest bed and the softest bedding. He'd quite appreciate it, I was certain.

Linx turned on me immediately, neighing in the soft, wuffly kind of way she did when she was confused.

"Hades has probably killed Persephone or done something to her body. The pantheon has sentenced him to purgatory of a sort." I lifted my hand. "I offered to keep him safe until they finished their inquiry into her disappearance."

To be honest, I wasn't quite certain Hades hadn't done it. Even I knew of the animosity between him and 'Sephone.

Did he do it?

I shrugged. "Maybe."

Then why did you bring him here? I thought you were simply supposed to fix our dead problem.

Giving her wide eyes, I thinned my lips. "I did fix our dead problem, Linx. I opened the gates."

She frowned prettily, causing her scales to glimmer like dusted emeralds in flame. *I ask you again, Calypso, why is he here? You did not need to bring him to fix our problem.*

At the time, it'd seemed like the thing to do. Especially with Dite whispering in my ear. Not to mention my sudden interest in intercourse and my fascination with Hades' broad shoulders and delicious rear.

"I want him. That is why."

You were pawing at him.

"I was claiming him. There's a difference." I sniffed.

I don't want him. She shook her head.

And I could only lift a brow, because it hadn't looked that way to me. "Well, I'm merely making sure he understands how things are going to work between us during his stay. He is my prisoner. I will sex him and then return him when his two weeks are up. I really do not see what the problem is here."

Linx's velvety nostrils flexed, and I could tell, after a lifetime together, that she had more to say but wasn't quite sure how to say it.

"Just tell me," I snapped, crossing my arms and beginning to get cross with her.

Only that I'm not sure that is the best way to engage his affections, Dear One.

"Oh," I laughed and batted a wrist, "is that all? I don't want his love, I just want his body."

Her frown grew deep. *Maybe you should go visit Nimue this evening. Speak to her about this situation and see what she has to say.*

Hm. Not a bad thought at all. Nimue was wise in the arts of men. I hadn't really thought to involve her in any of this, but now it seemed like a good idea.

"Yes, that is just what I shall do. But first, I'll eat a bite of lunch."

Nodding happily, Linx swam off to her stables, while I turned toward the kitchens in search of a quick bite.

I was just hugging a bowl of crab apples under my arm to go sit and eat them (I'd "borrowed" a few from Hades' orchard) when the water before me swirled a tinted pink color that sparkled with veins of glittering gold.

Knowing immediately who was reaching out to me, I took a bite of one crabby apple and blurted, "Proceed."

The water formed into the image of Dite. She was much prettier down here than in the Above. Her curves were no longer built of flesh but of water, and she shone like a pale-blue beacon.

The temple suddenly buzzed with life as glowworms crawled from out of their hiding holes to come and witness the rarely seen spectacle.

Aphrodite smiled, and I couldn't help but return it.

"What?" I asked around a mouthful. I wanted to visit with Nimue as soon as could be, and as much as I enjoyed Love's company, I had places to be.

"How goes the seduction, Caly?"

I shrugged. "Is that all you think about?"

Giving me wide eyes that clearly read "What do you think?" she nodded. "Of course."

"Fabulous." I swallowed my bite of apple, took another, swallowed that one too, and then grinned. "He sports quite an erection when around me. I think I should have my wicked way with him this evening."

She giggled, and I frowned.

"Oh, this should be fun, I've been waiting for the day that Hades was forced to yank the stick out of his ass."

I wasn't entirely sure what that had to do with me, but I said, "Mmhmm." Then, quickly switching subjects, I asked, "Any news regarding Persephone?"

"None yet." She shook her head. "It is like she and Cerberus vanished from the face of the earth. Apollo is scouring the grounds of Elysia as we speak. After that, he'll head into the Above while he still dominates the skies of Olympia."

"Hm, well, let us know."

"Will do." She seemed as though she meant to vanish, but with a small shake of her head, the Goddess of Love turned back to me. "Calypso, I'm well versed in matters of the heart. You should know that while Hades appears coarse and even at times cruel, he is lonely. More lonely than any one of us. Treat him kindly."

I'd had no intention of not treating him kindly. "I would think having sex every night would be a boon and not punishment, Dite."

"He is a man, darling. But that is not of what I speak. Be yourself with him. Do no other, beneath the hard exterior beats the heart of a man. Remember that."

That literally made no sense to me. But I nodded anyway.

"May I come and visit again?" she asked.

"Of course. But no other, I find the lot of you Olympians to be thoroughly disreputable."

Her tinkling laughter rolled through the waters, casting a dizzying spell on all that heard it.

With a gentle pop, Aphrodite vanished.

Smiling from ear to ear at this point, I downed three more apples, washed them down with a jar of honeyed mead, and drew a hand down my body., twisting my form yet again into the one Nimue was now familiar with, that of a scullery maiden who also happened to be one of Nim's very best friends.

Humming happily to myself, I made a mental note to ask Nim which position men liked best before our visit ended.

Chapter 4

Hades

I dropped my head into my hands. Here I was, sitting on the tongue of a massive clam, alone in a room that smelled heavily of flowery perfume and dripped with chains of pearls and prisms of radiant crystals that cut through walls of coral, and I wondered all over again if it'd been worth it.

I was used to the disdain of my family. Used to the side-eye glances and even, at times, disdainful looks.

I was Death.

I dealt in it.

Lived among it.

It was not a life I'd chosen for myself, but it was one I'd grown to respect and appreciate through the turning of the centuries. But to be so easily discarded, to be told that I could not return to my own realm, my people, made me seethe. Made me murderous.

I clenched my fists, breathing heavily.

I was a god, yes, but one against many. Alone, even I didn't stand a chance. My touch could not kill any of them. Hurt them, yes, if I choose it. With Cerberus by my side, I might have at least stood a chance of defending my gates, but with him gone, I'd known I'd had little choice but to submit.

The indignity of it infuriated me most.

Suddenly the pressure of the room tightened, as though the water were being suctioned up by a vacuum. I glanced up in time to see the waters spiral pink and then shimmer with gold.

Aphrodite stood before me as a pillar of water, her curves more luscious and sensuous than ever. The undulation of water had always held a strange fascination for me.

"What?" I snapped the instant she'd finished forming.

Planting hands on her hips, she gave me a kittenish pout. "Now, Death, is that any way to speak with a friend?"

"Why are you meddling here?" I asked, in no mood to play nice.

She rolled her eyes. "I should think it obvious. The two of you are snapping and sparking like a wildfire burning out of control."

I narrowed my eyes.

A gentle current swayed through the tips of her hair, causing them to swirl like charmed snakes around her face.

"And you just can't help yourself. Well, Love, I can assure you that the very last thought on my mind is engaging with Calypso. I have bigger problems."

She scoffed. "You're an idiot, Hades. Of course, I always thought you were. You had Persephone. You lost Persephone." She flicked a wrist. "You are lonely by your own doing."

She had no idea what she was talking about. I'd never wanted or asked for the other Olympians' friendship. They could go burn in Tartarus for all I cared.

Huffing, she crossed her arms in much the same pose Calypso had taken earlier, but somehow, it failed to make much of an impression on me.

"She is smitten with you."

"She is a virgin goddess. I hardly think—"

She snorted. "A problem she seeks to rectify immediately, I'd imagine. Look, Death." She curled her lip. "I recognize lust when I see it, and that woman plans to make you scream her name."

Chuckling because the thought actually made me not so angry at all, I leaned back on my hands in a relaxed pose. "I'd not kick her out of my bed."

Her eyes darted around the lush room. "Her bed. And you might find her to be a bit of a spitfire."

"I know this."

I vividly remembered the clawing at the back of my head with that kiss. Gods, that kiss. I almost groaned thinking about the salty, sweet taste of her tongue. The absolute power of her. She'd barely even given me a taste of it, she'd held so much of herself in check, but I'd be a liar if I said I hadn't craved much more than a sampling.

My groin tightened, but then I thought about the teases that Athena and Artemis were. How they made sport of making us sweat, making us males believe they'd be virgin goddesses no more, only to then turn around and mock and laugh at us for thinking we'd ever be good enough for either of them.

I glowered. "She's a cock tease and nothing more."

Her lips curled into a crooked smile, and her eyes twinkled like cut gems. "Whatever you say, Hades."

"Why are you here, Aphrodite? Answer me once and for all." I grew tired of her silly games and only wished my rest.

This day had been hell, and the next two weeks would only be worse. I knew they'd not find Persephone. All fingers would come pointing back at me, and a thousand years of torment was what awaited me.

I was tired and in a foul mood.

"Because I like her. And enthusiastic as she is, I do not think she quite knows what she's doing. When the rest of us took bodies, Calypso stayed in her primordial form, remaining so for almost her entire life. She knows little of how to be *human*," she finger quoted. "She is ancient, but in many ways she is naught more than a young woman—a young woman suddenly aware of her sexuality and her desire for relations. Be patient with her."

I frowned. I was very aware of her dichotomous nature, both the power that nestled inside her tempting body and the woman that spouted such nonsense I couldn't help but laugh in confusion.

She was both old and young. Her words were ridiculous. But her touch burned me to my very core. I'd not been touched the way she'd touched me in many lifetimes.

Blood rushed between my thighs at the thought of laying her down beneath me and filling her body with my heat and need.

I clenched my jaw. "In two weeks, I leave. I don't know what you expect me to do for her. If she does truly wish to shed her virginity, then perhaps she should consider one of the other gods."

But the thought of any of them—Zeus, Apollo, or even Poseidon (who'd once been her betrothed)—made me want to throttle them all and toss them into the River Styx.

Betrothal meant nothing to my kind. Zeus was married to Hera and still found time to sire at least a thousand bastards a year. Poseidon was rumored to be sleeping around with a bevy of selkies, and Apollo...well, he wasn't much competition. Unless Calypso suddenly sprouted a one-eyed snake, the God of the Sun would hardly notice.

Swiping my tongue across my lips, I still tasted a salty hint of her on them.

I glanced up when I felt the heavy press of Aphrodite's eyes. Her smile was broad.

"Do you not know, God of the Underworld, that still waters run deep? The sea can bring life and redemption. Remember that."

"Yes, and it can also drown a man." I thinned my lips.

She chuckled. "She is a tempestuous beauty, to be sure. But no one ever said falling in love with the Sea came without its share of hardships."

"Falling in love," I scoffed. "If she wishes to bed me, that I can accommodate, but nothing more."

She shrugged. "Your funeral. Anyway, beast, gotta jet. Hephy's making me eyeball stew for dinner. Mm." She rubbed her stomach, laughed, and disappeared in a glittering shower of gold dust.

"Bloody women."

Calypso

A hand grabbed my ass and squeezed.

I squeaked, jumping nearly off my tail fin at the rough treatment to my now-throbbing backside. Twirling, I nearly snapped the human man's hand off but then remembered I was in disguise.

Grinding my teeth, I gave the male a waspish smile. I knew him well. He was a troll of a man. One of the maidens had brought him down to sire a child late last year, but still they'd made no fry yet.

Jeffery, as he was called, was a short, round man with boring brown hair but pleasant-enough-colored eyes—a soft green, his most attractive feature to be sure—but he had the manners of a pig.

He was always sneaking about Nim's castle, harassing the staff.

"Jeffery," I snarled, "don't ye belong back wi' Merida? Last I checked, she were headin' for home."

Jeffery, the scoundrel, smiled a pudgy-cheeked smile and shrugged. "She can do as she pleases."

He had a willing maiden and yet here he was, day in and day out. I hadn't mentioned him to Nim yet, mainly because while he was a rat, the man was harmless. But now he was annoying me.

I aimed to teach him manners and didn't want my daughter-in-law involved in what would surely be a bloody affair. Bruce, I was sure, was quite hungry today, my poor little beastie.

My head was full of visions of evisceration when the doors of the kitchen were flung open and a heavily pregnant Nimue waddled in.

My heart was full to bursting to see her thus. I'd never dreamed that someday I'd actually become a grandmother. I'd felt the life pulse of the babes and knew something my Nim did not.

She was having twins. One boy, one girl. One would only ever have human form, but the boy, the boy was a changeling. The first mer-male born since Sircco eons ago.

Of course, I couldn't tell her these things, as she had no idea who I really was, and then the peg would be up, as they say.

Was it peg? Oh well, whatever.

As she swiped at her long hair, Nimue's eyes found mine immediately.

"Janita!" She smiled serenely.

The pregnancy had her fair skin glowing like porcelain. She'd already been lovely, and now I could only find her doubly so.

"You are here. I'd hoped you worked a shift today."

I curtsied quickly. "Consort."

Her smile quickly vanished, however, when she spotted Jeffrey. A twitch of her eyebrow was enough to make the vermin scuttle off.

My Nim was steely to the core. Human she might be, but pirate's blood ran through her veins, and the power of the Sea was at her disposal. No man was fool enough to mess with her.

Grabbing my hands, she gave them a quick squeeze once Rat Face had gone. "I'm famished, and I'd hoped to find you here."

Grinning, I turned and lifted a basket of food from the coral counter, dangling it happily before her.

There were perks to being me, namely that with a mere thought, I could create a masterpiece of foods. None in the kitchens knew that my divine creations hadn't truly been made by my hands. I was a master at remaining hidden when I wished to be.

"I've made all your favorites, Consort. Mashed cod with parsley flakes. Steaming lobster bisque, and kelp drop biscuits."

"Mm." She groaned, rubbing her massive belly. "I hope you brought some for yourself."

I chuckled. "I've already eaten, my lady."

"Well then." She latched her arm through mine. "Come join me as I devour this sumptuous feast."

Glancing at the rest of the staff, she nodded her head.

Every maiden within Seren had fallen prey to Nim's charms. She simply had that effect on others. I was well pleased with my son's chosen consort.

In the hall, we passed Sircco. I glanced off, pretending to straighten an already straight picture frame on the wall.

"Beluga," Nim murmured his name softly but with a wealth of love behind it.

I fought my grin. I thought that tonight, while I was drowning Apollo's mansion in saltwater and extracting my revenge on Jeffery the rat, I might spare a moment to surprise my children with a little bauble. Nim was rather fond of my golden pearls.

Sircco wrapped her in his arms, nuzzling the side of her neck, and I experienced a soft pang of longing.

I wanted sex because of what they had.

I wanted the intimacy of their shared words. The union of their souls. How they seemed to innately know the thoughts and wants of the other.

"Are you to sup, then?" he asked her softly.

She nodded, brushing at a curl of hair on his cheek. "Yes. Will I, um...see you later?"

I was now pretending to dust off my tail. They were meeting up for sex. See, sex was wonderful. How could I not want that?

He tried to mask his answer by whispering it in her ear, but nothing was hidden to me within my waters.

"As long as you promise to wear those wicked fishnet stockings you found the other day."

Fishnet stockings? What in the world were those? And how could I get my hands on some?

She tittered. It was really rather adorable. And then, with a gentle swat to her rear, Sircco swam off, acknowledging me briefly with a short dip of his head.

"King." I curtsied.

Nim's arm was once again threaded through mine, and before I knew it, she'd dragged me into their massive dining chambers, which we had all to ourselves, as was the case these days.

Nimue had decreed that she wished to take her lunches alone. But for some odd reason, she always allowed me in on her private time.

"Sit." She pointed to the seat beside hers at the head of the long driftwood table.

I sat, twiddling my thumbs as she began to unpack her basket of goods. I smiled as her eyes grew big. Holding a fork in each hand, she looked like a child as she gazed longingly at each plate.

"I hardly know where to start. You spoil me rotten, Janita."

"Ah, it were nuthin', m'lady." I batted away her words while inside, I beamed.

She happily munched for a while, and I didn't interrupt her. I wished her to eat her fill. She had my twins to care for, after all.

But once she began grazing, I figured she'd eaten as much as her stomach could hold, and I spoke up. "My lady?"

"Hm?" She looked up, finally setting down her forks. She'd very nearly demolished all three plates of food. What could have easily fed four had just barely been enough for one very ripe consort.

"I wish to speak frankly, if I may."

"Of course, Janita. You know you can tell me anything you wish."

I dipped my head. "Thank you."

Suddenly nervous, I drummed my fingers and swished my tail back and forth. I wasn't a complete novice when it came the idea of men, but there was so much about them that felt lacking to me.

Swallowing a deep breath, I rushed out, "I've found myself a male."

"Oh." Her rosebud lips quirked into a small "o." "That is wonderful. Is he handsome?"

My eyes widened with enthusiasm. "Excessively. He is—" I almost said his name and then realized that would open me up to far too many questions "—lovely. He's got great, wide hands." I splayed mine open. "Fingers that can really grip my arse, you know."

She pressed her lips together, then gave a small cough before waving her hand. "Bone. It is nothing, continue."

I frowned. I never left fish bones in my meals.

As if realizing my thoughts, she was quick to say, "Oh, no, not from your food, dear. Cook fried me up a plate of fish earlier, and I've been coughing all morning trying to get it loose."

I thwacked her back hard at least three times.

She grunted, falling forward and planting her hands on the table.

"Good?" I asked, ready to thwack her again if she should need it.

"Oh no," she looked up at me with eyes now watering and gave me a thumbs up. "I think you got it for sure."

Nim cleared her throat, grunted, and then nodded. "Yup, definitely gone now."

"Good. So anyway," I sighed, "he's hawt."

She laughed. "That's the best kind. What are his lips like?"

I brushed fingers over my own. They were soft and sensitive, but I remembered what his had felt like. Hard, claiming, dominating. "They are fuller on the bottom than the top. But he knows how to work them well, if that's what you mean. My body turned to lava when he touched me."

"Oh my. Tell me more."

I smiled, setting farther into my chair. "Well, I wish to claim him tonight. I want to straddle his cock and ride him till the morning, that is."

She choked again, and I lifted my hand, but she quickly shook her head. "No, I'm good, love. I'm good."

"Are you sure? Fish bones can be quite tricky."

"Quite. But I'm all for riding a lovely cock. What exactly is the matter? Because I sense you have a question."

I drummed my fingers. "What are fishnets, and why do men like them?"

"Ah. I see." Leaning back in her seat, she rubbed her belly a few times before saying, "Men are visual creatures by nature. You don't really have to do much to excite them. Just show up, preferably naked, and they're like putty in your hands."

"Mmhm." I nodded, deep in thought. But that still didn't explain why Sircco wanted her in fishnets. "But—"

She held up a finger. "You clearly overhead my king referring to my fishnets."

I didn't blush. Why should I? There were no secrets uttered within my waters I did not know. I shrugged.

"You see, when a couple has been together for a while as the King and I have, sometimes we wish to get creative to keep the spark alive." Glancing over her shoulder, she leaned forward and whispered, "Sircco and I play games all the time. Sometimes I tie him up to my bed and give him a few lashes to rev him."

"Wow." I breathed. "And he doesn't get angry about that?"

She laughed. "Not with the types of lashes I gave him. It's important that for every sting there is also something tender to help ease the pain. He generally likes a gentle rub or a kiss."

"Mm. Yes, I could see where that might work." I imagined Hades stretched out before me with a whip in my hand, and I felt such a flutter of white-hot need that it was an effort to remain in my seat much longer.

"But not all men enjoy that type of game. You have to figure out what your man enjoys, Janita."

Feeling a little as though I'd just been shot back to square one, I glowered. "And how am I to know what he likes?"

"Ask him."

"Ask him?" I snapped my fingers. "Just like that?"

"Yes, of course. Just like that." She winked. "Believe me, men are quite willing to talk about sex. It's one of their favorite pastimes, after all."

"Mine too. When I finally have it, that is," I said dreamily then looked up at her. "What type of questions should I ask? I've seen men and women ride each other like mules. I'd imagine he'd like that."

"Oh yes, I'm sure so."

"And I saw a woman once stick a carrot up her man's—"

She cleared her throat again as a fierce blush rose to her cheeks. "I can imagine. And you never know, your man may like that, too."

I nodded. "Okay, so I ask him. Got it."

"Buy yourself a few outfits. Play dress-up for him. Men usually like that."

"What kinds?" I really should have brought a notepad, there was so much information to remember.

"Well, pirates are a fantasy for some. I happen to have some great clothes if you need any."

We were about the same size—prepregnancy, that was. I was just about to ask her for some when I realized that technically she thought I had a tail and wouldn't need a skirt or pants, but I couldn't imagine simply walking up to Hades with only a top on and my pearl exposed to the world.

But then again...

"In fact," she clapped her hands, and almost instantly a maid appeared.

"Yes, m'lady." The chubby maid with coal-black hair dipped low.

"Buella, can you please run to my chambers and pick out a set of my old pirate clothes. The best set I have, the um...magenta and gold one, I think," Nim said after eyeing me a quick second.

"Yes, mum." Buella was gone in an instant.

Nimue turned back to me with a smile. "It'll only take a minute. I do hope that once you're done sexing him up, you'll bring him by to meet us, love. We would all very much enjoy meeting the man finally good enough for our Janita."

I laughed. "Oh, I'm not sure about good enough. He's thoroughly disreputable and debauched, which makes him absolutely perfect for me."

Our grins matched.

Buella returned only a few moments later carrying a wrapped bundle in her hand.

"Set it just there, Buella, thank you." Nim pointed at my spot on the table.

The maiden set it down, curtsied one final time, and then swam off.

Pushing back my chair, I dipped my head at the Consort. "Well, I'm to shove off now. I do believe my work here is done."

"Oh, yes, go shove off." Nim tapped her jaw. "And remember, have fun."

Grabbing the package, I nodded. "Oh, and one last thing before I forget. I like you very much, Nimue. Truly. Frogs of a feather we are."

She cleared her throat again before giving me the thumbs up. "Yes, we are, Janita. Now go make your debauched male thoroughly happy."

Chapter 5

Nimue

Sircco returned to my side the moment "Janita" left. Wrapping me up in his arms, he kissed me softly. We broke apart with a happy little sigh. Then, signaling to me with his finger on his lips, he created a pocket of air around us, a bubble that safely encased us and made it impossible for anything or any*one* to listen in on our conversation.

"What did that old stingray want this time?" he chuckled.

The laughter I'd fought so hard to contain during her visit came pouring out of me in great, heaving sobs, leaving me feeling dizzy and breathless.

"Oh, gods, your mother has secured her a man."

He snorted then joined me in laughter. "Good gods. She is adorable."

"Aye, she is. Though I do believe she honestly thinks she has us all hoodwinked by her maiden disguise."

"Well," he slipped his fingers through my hair, hair that'd grown out past my bum at this point, "I do think she's got most of them fooled. Mother, though naïve in many ways, is no fool. I think we see through her because we know her so well, and so few of us do. It is an honor, truly. I'm just grateful she likes you."

"Tut." I patted his cheek. "I tamed her as I've tamed all fish. She loves me and I her, and I do hope that whoever this male is, he will survive the tempest that is your mother."

"Oh, gods, for all our sakes." He stifled a chuckle. Then, lifting my hands to his lips, he kissed my knuckles tenderly. "Now, about those fishnets..."

Calypso

I was horny.

And tired.

But mostly I just wanted to get on with things already.

Marching through my halls, I spotted no one about. Which was good, as I was not in the mood to entertain idle tittle-tattle. The package was burning a hole through my hands.

I was desperate to unwrap it and see just what surprises Nimue had packed for me.

Unable to resist the curiosity a moment longer, I hurriedly switched forms, debating whether to go to Hades as a woman of flesh or water and decided that I should do both.

I'd heard once that the play of hot and cold could be terribly sexually stimulating. I was a fully formed woman, but the right half of me was built of water.

To be sure, I probably looked bizarre, but there was beauty to it, too. The limbs of water sparkled like diamond dust in the noonday sun. My hair hung long and loose down my backside, exposing the tiny dimples just above my bum line. I had a banging body.

With a contented little sigh, I undid the wrapping and cooed at the exquisite feel of glowworm silk.

The outfit Nimue had gifted me with was a very fine stitching. The silk had been dyed opposing and yet beautifully complementary colors. I quickly pulled the top over my head and cinched the lacing behind my back.

There was a good five inches of bare skin left bare. I smiled, ready to walk into that room with my goods exposed and have my naughty way with Death Boy, when I spied what appeared to be a lace skirt and a dainty pair of black lace stockings.

The silly maid had obviously forgotten that I was naught but a mere maiden with no legs.

Thankfully, though, I did have legs, and so her oversight would now prove to be a boon.

I quickly slipped on the skirt and gasped at the decadent feel of such lush fabric but also at the provocative garment. The skirt was shredded up the sides so that each time I stepped, a long expanse of thigh would be bared. That, coupled with the stockings, which bore markings of sea roses (my favorite aquatic flower), had me feeling decidedly wicked.

There was also a golden chain much too long for my neck, so I wrapped it around my exposed waist. It jingled as I walked. I also found a pair of high-heeled boots.

"How in the bloody hell does Nim walk in these?" I eyed the ridiculously long length of heel—easily four inches and coming to a very narrow point at the end. But I had to admit that once I slipped them on, they made my slender ankles and softly muscled calves look fabulous.

The finishing touch was a pirate's hat, a black thing that curled up on one side and had a cream-white sash tied around it that trailed down my spine.

"Mirror." I snapped my fingers. Instantly the waters before me turned into a looking glass from floor to ceiling. Twirling, I checked myself out.

My ass looked perfect.

My breasts were like lovely, ripe melons.

And my face was flawless.

"Who wouldn't want me?" I smiled, and with a kick of the strange heels I was coming to adore, I turned and made for the room.

I didn't knock. I didn't even utter a word. I simply opened the doors a moment later, snapped my fingers, and in an instant, Hades was undressed and chained to a four-poster bed. I'd considered using my clam bed, as I was accustomed to its softness, but there'd been no way to shackle him to it.

"Calypso!" he grunted, writhing and twisting his magnificent body, his gorgeous face red with sudden fury and shock. "What is the meaning of this?"

Bracing my feet wide, I waited for him to stop being such a grumpy ass and look at me.

He did only a moment later, and his jaw dropped.

Smirking, I let him study me as I devoured him.

He was brilliant, his body corded and tight with ropey muscle. His shapely chest rose and fell while his stomach contracted with his breath, causing his abdominals to flex and strain.

I frowned to note he was covered in slash marks from the bottom of his chin to just above the dark thatch of curls between his legs.

But I soon forgot about the scars at the sight of his lovely cock. Long and veiny, the color of his flesh reminded me of wet sand.

I couldn't seem to stop sighing, especially once that turgid member rose to greet me.

He cleared his throat. "Calypso, release me."

I pouted. I wanted to keep looking at him, not talking. "Hades, I mean to sex you. Why ever would I release you? You forget you are my prisoner for the next two weeks. I keep you as I want you, and I want you as you are."

Wetting my lips, I stepped inside, and the doors slammed behind me with the rush of a sudden current. The water smelled of flowers but was now also scented with the rising thrum of our desires.

He wanted me as I wanted him.

I trailed fingers along the tops of my breasts, playing in the vee between them as though unaware of his sudden, harsh intake of breath.

Hades

One moment I'd been contemplating asking someone for food, the next I was chained to a bed and treated to a sight I'd never believed possible, not in a million years.

Calypso was staring at me as though she meant to devour me. The thought only made me feel hotter.

She was more beautiful than I could have imagined, a mixture of woman and magic. Even the fleshy side of her sparkled with light. I wanted to yank that hat off her head, toss it to the floor, and run my fingers through her soft green hair.

I should be furious with her. Never in my life had a woman treated me as she did now.

But maybe that was part of her appeal. She was unlike anything I'd ever come across before.

Letting my eyes linger at the swell of her breast, I wet my lips. "Take off your clothes, imp."

She grinned. "That is not how this works, Dead Boy. I sex you, not the other way around."

I narrowed my eyes. I would let her have her way with me. What red-blooded male could deny her? But I would lay ground rules.

"Tonight only. Tonight you can have your way with me. I am yours to please. But tomorrow it is my turn."

"No. I reject that proposal."

I lifted my brow. Temperamental goddess. "Then you do not get to play with me, Calypso. I am a god, too, and I can deny you."

She bit her bottom lip. A lush, red bottom lip. A lip I desperately wanted to taste again.

Calypso knew I was right. I could deny her. I wouldn't. It seemed to me that sex was not such a bad thing right now, but I had to make her believe she did not hold all the cards. I was an ancient, too, and knew that if I let her manipulate me once, the cycle would never end. That was a mistake I'd made once in my life; never again.

Pouting prettily, she stomped her foot, causing her luscious breasts to jiggle. By the gods, I could not really believe this was happening. A virgin goddess gifting me her greatest treasure.

I trembled at the thought.

She sidled close to my side, close enough that she was now leaning over me and trailing a finger down my left rib cage. It was all I could do to clamp down on my moan. I was so hard I felt I might burst.

The drought had been long, far too long for me.

"Hades," she whispered as she circled one of my nipples.

I bucked under her touch, clenching my teeth, determined not to let her see just how desperate I was now becoming.

"You know you want to play."

Squeezing my eyes shut, I thought of Aphrodite's words. Calypso was more ancient even than the Titans. She was a primordial, which actually made her older than me. But she'd not been human long, so it might be possible to use her newfound enthusiasm to my advantage.

"You wish to know sex? True sex? Correct?"

Her finger stopped moving, and a cold, calculating look moved through her sea-blue eyes. "Why do you ask?"

"Because I am not without knowledge. You do to me as you wish this night, and tomorrow I show you more of the carnal arts."

"Only tomorrow?"

I grinned. She was naïve but smart. "No, not only tomorrow. We take turns. Whatever you wish from me on your nights, I will do. Likewise, whatever I wish from you on my nights, you will do."

She hissed, clamping her hand to my neck in a punishing grip. The waters between us swirled and raged, causing her hair to lash my eyes.

"Do you play me for a fool, Hades!"

I remained as I was, even though I had the power to make her release me with naught but a thought. For too long I'd been cold, dead inside, and Calypso was like a spark to my soul. An ember I'd not thought I had anymore was suddenly flaring to life. She excited my passions, but she needed to agree to my terms on this. On that I would not budge.

"Tell me, Sea, why did you save me this day?" I asked her calmly.

Immediately the rage lessened and the waters cooled. My tempestuous captor was living up to her name.

She shrugged. "I wished to know you, Hades."

"Sexually?" I lifted a brow.

She paused for a moment, long enough that I noticed. Was she wishing for more than mere sex? I'd never even considered that a possibility, but her words quickly brushed off my thoughts.

"Of course. You're a beautiful male specimen. I wish to shed this baggage." She pointed between her legs. "You will do."

"You speak so strangely, my dear."

She laughed. "Am I your dear already? Oh my, I guess my feminine wiles are much more powerful than I'd imagined."

I stared deep into her eyes, entranced by the hypnotic sway of her figure, the way the water literally seemed to breathe in her. If she only knew.

"Parley."

I frowned. "What?"

"I concede, you fool. Do not ask me to release you from this prison. And if I say no to sex, you must stop, but if I like your suggestion, then *arrrrr*," she twitched her lips and pumped her arm, "I'll do it."

"What was that?" I shook my head.

Giving me wide eyes, as though I were too stupid to live, she brushed a hand down her voluptuous body. "I'm a pirate. I am being a pirate. Is this not obvious, Hades?"

I laughed.

For a moment I thought perhaps I shouldn't have when an angry light flashed like twin bolts through her eyes, but soon the anger turned to something else entirely.

Humming beneath her breath, she palmed both her hands to my chest and raked delicately.

The fire of desire lit through me like a powder keg ready to burst. I sucked in air like a bellows and hissed.

"Are you ready for sex now or what?" She bent over me, her teeth nipping at my earlobe.

"Good gods," I groaned. "No foreplay. No sweet nothings, no—"

Gripping my shaft tight in her hands, she fisted me. I expected her not to have a clue what to do with me, as she was untried. A virgin mother, she'd never lain with another soul, but she did not at all act like a novice.

Calypso had obviously studied well.

"No," she snipped. Then, standing, she released me, and I wanted to beg her to pump me again.

Reaching between her legs, she ripped at a hole in the stockings and, with a wicked glint in her eyes, straddled my hips, her hot center resting just at the throbbing tip of me.

"Bloody hell," I groaned when she sank down on me.

I'd expected flowery, girly nonsense, weeping and whimpering, and a woman who had no idea what to do.

Calypso sank down on me deep, clenching me in her tight, wet channel, and I could only grunt as the light from her body reflected off the walls like a giant prism.

I wanted to grab her waist, wanted to pin her down and slam into her, but she held me prisoner and rode me like a woman possessed.

She never undressed, never did more than grunt and wiggle her hips, taking me in slow and deep, and I thought I would die from the pleasure.

I closed my eyes for a second, lost to the swirling madness of the moment, to the heady scent of our bonding. When next I opened them, she was staring at me not with the innocence of an untried maiden but with eyes now dripping with revelation.

"Oh, Hades," she moaned and trembled violently, the quaking of her inner muscles milking an orgasm from me.

"Calypso!" I roared my release.

Chapter 6

Calypso

Thoroughly spent, I patted his chest and, with one final wiggle of my hips, bounced off him.

I felt I could fly.

I wanted to have more sex, truth be told. But he was giving me an odd look I wasn't sure I liked.

"Well, that'll do, I suppose." With a flick of my fingers, I released him from his shackles. "You may go now. Take any room in the temple and sleep well, Death Boy."

He frowned, glancing down at his now clothed body. The dark pants were a little more snug between his legs than was usual. And the top button of his black silk shirt was opened wide enough to give me a tantalizing peek at the hollow of his throat.

By the gods, the man was sexy.

"That's it?" he snapped, riffling fingers through his hair.

At first I thought he might have been angry with me, but then he tipped his head back and laughed, the sound of it reaching toward the rafters and shaking the very foundation of coral my temple rested upon.

My lips twitched, rather liking the sound of it.

"Of course that's it. Did you expect sweet nothings from me? My dear boy, I am not that kind of girl."

Eyes like purest obsidian gleamed back at me. "I should feel used, Calypso."

I sighed, making sure my breasts heaved for dramatic effect. His eyes zeroed in on the sight with a quickness that branded my very flesh with hot pricklings of need.

My stomach swirled. I wanted to rip his pants off him and do it again. I loved sex. It'd been most enjoyable.

But I would not sate my newfound desire with him again tonight. Relationships were complicated and messy, tragic things doomed to fail. Except, of course, for Nim and Sircco. I'd see anyone hanged if they tried to interfere with those two.

They, however, were the exception to the rule. I'd done the whole engagement thing with Seidy, who I affectionately referred to as Psycho when he wasn't looking. No thank you.

Even Dite with her passion for her twisted male slept around. I'm sure Hephy would, too, if anyone would have him, that was.

Standing, I suffered a very odd and strange emotion. Nothing and no one cowed me, ever. But when the massive wall of muscle and beauty that was Hades stood toe to toe with me, I felt suddenly small and delicate.

It was the strangest sensation, this desire I suddenly had to lean into his chest and rest my cheek upon him and maybe listen to his heart beat.

Surely the sound of it would be like *A Night on Bald Mountain* by Mussorgsky: menacing and brooding and macabrely wonderful.

But I did none of those things. I locked my eyes with his. "If you mean to intimidate me, Reaper, you've got another think coming."

His brow twitched, and then he drew his knuckle down my cheek. Just a small, feathery touch, but it burned straight through me and made me shiver.

"You fascinate me, Thalassa."

I sucked in a breath. I hadn't been called by that name in ages, since before the dawn of man. It was my true birth name.

Swallowing hard, for once I had no words to say, and I watched hungrily as he turned and strode from my room.

I wanted to chase after him. Wanted to call him back and demand he tell me why he'd said that name. But goddesses did not beg.

Glaring at my now open bedroom door, I debated whether it was a good idea to release the tsunami of violence I barely kept in check within me.

But then I thought of Nim's precious sea snail garden and swallowed my urge. She would not thank me for destroying her yearly crop.

But there was one way I could assuage my sudden thirst for destruction. Closing my eyes, I channeled all my confusion and rage into two cognizant thoughts.

"Apollo and Jeffery."

Cackling to myself, I gathered the waters of the deep, filling them with all the filth of litter legger fools had selfishly dropped into them, and shot them out like twin harpoons.

In my head I saw Jeffery sputter as a rolling wave snatched him up, keeping him under as he struggled mightily to escape the very sudden and quite unexpected (oops) riptide.

His sea maiden, well aware that the waters had been sent by moi, did not interfere. I should drown his miserable rat ass for being such a fool. But I was turning over a new leaf now.

So I only let him suffer for a little while. Just until his face turned blue and his eyes began to bulge from a lack of breathable water.

He collapsed to his hut floor a mere second later, hacking and spluttering and drooling all over himself.

"Pathetic legger." I curled my lip.

But then I smiled when I turned my gaze toward Apollo's shimmering temple that now dripped with brine, salt, and yards and yards of slimy kelp, not to mention several gallons' worth of litter.

"Calypso!" Apollo roared, obviously well aware it'd been me and not Psycho who'd done it. I shrugged. Apollo held no dominion over me. The lights that lit Seren were of my own making, an enchantment similar to the sun, but not actually sun at all.

There was nothing the golden-haired narcissist could do to me down here. In fact, there was nothing any of the miserable pantheon could do to me. I was far greater in power than they were, and they all knew it.

Dusting my hands off, I twirled, feeling strangely...lonely.

Curling my nose in disgust, because the Goddess of the Sea was *never* in want of company, I vanished this ridiculous outfit with a thought.

Well, not entirely ridiculous. I might need to use it again; Hades had practically wet himself for want of me. But that heat had soon turned to something else when he'd orgasmed. There'd been a softness to him, one I'd not expected.

One that intrigued me far more than most anything else we'd done tonight.

Laughing, I shook my head. I was becoming a maudlin fool in my old age.

Wishing to be rid of this body, I returned to my natural state. Instantly my thoughts eased as I felt the hum of life, of my children move through me. Bruce was several hundred feet away and gorging on the bloated carcass of a bucktoothed whale.

Nim and Sircco were...oh, I shut off the channel. Best to give them their privacy.

Most of my maidens were with their chosen bedmates for the evening. Psycho was banging a bevy of porpoises at the same time.

He really was a pervert. Why bang twenty when you could bang one for life?

Hm. Where had that thought come from?

Life was such a long time for ones such as us.

All around me, I felt the yawn and breath of life and death. Death was a part of my world, and I accepted it as such. Very few things lived forever. There was a natural cycle to life and a beauty to death few souls could ever truly appreciate.

To live a life well, to have no regrets, be you fish, maiden, or even a damnable legger. To close your eyes and know that there was peace in the beyond and to smile because now the pain would soon be over and there'd be nothing more beyond that but joy.

Yes, there was beauty in death.

Thinking of death obviously turned my thoughts to the man himself, the collector of legger souls.

He'd told me I fascinated him.

Truth was, he fascinated me too.

I felt him as he paced the length of the room beside my own, his lips pulled down, his thoughts pensive and weighty. He stared at nothing, but his thoughts were clearly heavy and distracting.

Why was he not sated? Had I not pleasured him well? Was there more I should have done? Maybe the carrot?

But I quickly banished the thoughts and stopped spying on him. Whatever his thoughts were, they were his own.

There'd been guilt etched onto his face. Around the corners of his eyes. Hades knew Persephone's fate. The scales of justice would move as they must.

Needing the comfort of a friend, I flashed to where Linx was stabled.

The hippocampus lifted her glittering head, sensing my presence immediately.

Sister? Why are your thoughts so heavy?

I honestly was not sure. I was a virgin no more, and that should have been cause for celebration. Instead, I wrapped my form around Linx's body and hugged her tight.

She let me do it, not moving an inch the rest of the night as I fitfully slept.

Hades

"Please Hades, if you ever cared for me at all, don't do this," Persephone pleaded, clenching her fingers tight.

Hades stared in fury. How dare she? How dare she demand of him further?

He'd given her everything. Spoiled her even. For so long, all he'd wanted was her love, but he'd soon learned that Persephone loved nothing so well as herself.

He'd have settled for respect at the very least, but even that she'd withheld.

Lifting a hand, he glared at her. He was powerful. A god. She could not do to him what he did not allow. But he'd always been weak to her wiles. Until the day he wasn't. Until the burden of her yearly visits made him want to weep and gnash his teeth with disgust and vexation.

Hades had tried to end their arrangement, but the terms had been sealed by the Fates, and unless one were willing to take her place, he'd never be able to undo what'd been wrought by a zealous fit of passion nearly an eternity ago.

Her eyes flashed. "You won't do this. You won't because you still love me."

He scoffed. "I do not love you, you little fool. My love for you has turned to hate. After what you've done to Cerberus, do you think I could ever forgive this!"

She laughed. Literally laughed in his face. Any pretense at kindness faded quickly. "That mangy mutt will grow it back. No real harm done. But if you do this, I swear to the gods, they will see you burn for this."

He moved as though to strike her but held back at the last moment. He hated her, but at his core, Hades was now and would always be a gentleman.

"I despise your black soul," she scoffed, lifting her chin. "Hit me, you beast. Hit me hard!"

Shaking her by the shoulders, he roared, "Stop this at once!"

"You deserve nothing less! Now let me go—"

He moved. A tangle of limbs. Cerberus snapping one of his massive jaws, and then there was nothing more but pools of blood...

Gasping, I sat up, clutching at my chest. The dream left me shaken—and utterly destroyed, because it'd been no dream.

It'd all happened.

"Damn her to Tartarus!" I roared, kicking off the sheets and staring at the golden walls of the room with hate, fury, and the injustice of it all.

If I talked, I was damned. If I didn't talk, I was damned.

There would be no out for me from this. None.

Calypso had given me a short reprieve for her own selfish ends. As with most others, she was no different. She'd taken what she'd wanted—my body; she cared naught about the rest.

Turning on my heel, I stopped, staring broodily at the diamond-dipped clam-shell bed I'd slept on, the sea kelp that climbed like vines up the walls and glimmered like green and blue neon. The room was both gaudy and tasteful.

A strange mix of excess and beauty.

Like the woman herself.

Sighing, I dropped down onto the edge of the bed. I did not hate her. In fact, Calypso had been a breath of fresh air for me. When I was with her, I didn't think about Persephone or what she'd done to me.

What I'd done to her.

She'd grown out of hand. And no matter how many times I'd talked of that with Demeter, she'd refused to hear me out. Refused to believe it.

So I'd done what I'd done, and though I had no regrets, I felt the injustice of their judgment keenly.

Clenching my jaw, I hung my head.

There was a soft glow coming in from the window. Apollo did not actually track across the waters here, so whatever this light was, the enchantment came from Calypso herself.

I'd visited Poseidon's grotto once. It'd been a bachelor's paradise, with a bevy of nude sirens and sea creatures to warm his bed. Poseidon's waters catered to nothing but the carnal.

Calypso's, on the other hand, teemed with actual life. With citizens that lived and breathed and worked and loved. She'd built a true utopia in this Below, and had I been brought here under different circumstances, I might have enjoyed it more.

I snorted as a sudden flash of memory ripped through my thoughts: her in that bizarre costume, riding me like I was a stallion, with her head tossed back and a look of wonder in her eyes.

A wild, witchy, enchantress.

In so many ways, Calypso was a mystery to not just me but all the Pantheon. Water was the essence of life. All peoples of all nations and tongues worshipped her, even without ever uttering a prayer. Without water, life would cease to exist.

Because of that, she was a great power and, should she ever wish it, a threat to Zeus's reign.

Poseidon was also a water deity, but he'd been born long after her. No, the true power had always lain with Calypso—Thalassa, as I was coming to think of her—but she'd always been a shy, absent creature, content to live out her days as a hermit and so often overlooked by those of us on Olympus.

I grinned, wondering at a world in which she reigned and we no longer did, and I found it not to be such a terrible thing.

My position would always be secure. She was life. I was death. One could not exist without the other. But many of the Pantheon were antiquated beings with ideals no longer suitable to this day and age.

Just then, the door was thrown open, and a maiden I'd never seen before swam inside.

Her hair was a silvery gray, and though her face was more mature, she was not in the least bit old. She was rather attractive, sturdy and solidly built with sharp features that, separately, weren't entirely pleasing but together created a symmetrical harmony. A tail the same shade as her hair swished as she swam inside.

"'Ello, Master Hades, and 'ow are you this fine mornin'?"

Blue eyes the shade of a clear spring sky smiled back at me.

There was something about her movements, the expert precision to them, and the lithe sway of her body that caught my attention instantly.

In her hands she carried a wooden tray brimming with food. Biscuits. Fruit. Cheeses. Nuts. I sniffed, instantly scenting the honeyed mead in the smoking stoneware pot.

"I'm fine, Miss—" I paused, awaiting her name.

Bobbing cutely, she said, "Janita. The name's Janita. I'm about to hie meself off to the king's palace for the day, but the goddess wished to see you fed well."

Leaning back on my hands, I watched as she set the tray down on the nightstand.

"Did she? Give your mistress my thanks."

She nodded, nibbling on her luscious bottom lip and looking far more nervous now that she no longer carried a tray. Her eyes darted toward the door and then back to me at least three times.

Clearly she knew she should leave but wasn't quite ready to do it yet.

"Something you wish, Janita?"

She cleared her throat. "Well, it's only that the mistress weren't sure what types of food ye liked, ye see. And um...tomorrow she'd like to pleasure you." She shook her head. "No, that's not the right word. Please you, please you. Aye."

I thinned my lips, entertained mightily.

"Does she? How kind."

She picked her thumbnail. "Well?"

Snapping my fingers, I called the tray over to my side and began to nibble on the cheeses first. The golden squares had a nutty, sweet taste.

"The cheese is very pleasing," I murmured. "Though I'm not fond of nuts." I pushed that plate aside.

"Yes, yes." She bobbed her head. "And the fruit?"

I shrugged, picking at the bowl of figs. "I'm partial to pomegranates."

"Oh, right, of course." She smacked her forehead. "I knew that. Erm, I mean, because of the stories and such."

"Bread is okay," I pressed on, as though I'd not heard her. "And of course," I lifted the steaming pot full of mead, "I like mead, but I'm most partial to ambrosia."

After I finished complaining about nearly every item on the tray, her eyes turned a frosty blue. "Is that all?"

Smirking, I stood, towering over her invading her space. I was impressed that she didn't back up. A lesser woman would have.

"Tell your mistress that what I most prefer is naught but a simple repast of toast and coffee. That'll do."

Turning on my heel, I dismissed her and busied myself with the food. It all looked good, actually. I wondered if Calypso had made it with her own hands.

Suddenly I was bowled over by a wave and pinned to the bed with my cheek pressed to the mattress. The pressure relented after only a moment. Clearing my throat, I stood and dusted myself off.

"You've quite the temper, maiden," I spoke coolly.

Lovely Janita seethed. "I'll have you know, dil-do, the *mistress* worked all morning creating those for you. The least you could do was show a little courtesy."

I was quite certain she'd not meant to call me a dildo; however, with her, nothing was quite impossible, either.

Pouring on the charm, an act I so rarely attempted, as I had grown bored with my kind, I once more invaded her sphere, this time making certain to brush a very hard part of my anatomy against her tail.

She trembled and then shivered when my hands trailed languidly up her bare forearms.

"Well then, my lovely little maiden, do me the honor of telling your *mistress*," I lowered my head, so that our noses practically touched, "thank you."

She clutched at her lip with her sharp little teeth. And when her tongue poked out, it was all I could do not to lean in and snatch it up for my own.

"O...okay," she murmured docilely. But I wasn't fooled. This angel had horns.

Standing back, I released her. And fought a grin when she stumbled forward a minute inch. Her hands were aflutter around her head as she tucked strands of hair behind her ears.

Curtseying, she made as though to go.

"Oh, and Janita, one last thing," I said as she was halfway out the door.

Clutching at the frame with one clawed hand, she whispered, "Aye?"

"Tell, Calypso, tonight is my night and this time it will be she and not I that screams."

She gulped and I thought for certain she would leave me then. But she did not. Squaring her shoulders, she said, "You know who I really am, don't you?"

Feeling foolishly relaxed, I walked over to her. Her eyes were so blue and wide. Shaped like a doe's. In any form she came, I could not seem to pull my gaze away.

Pulling a fistful of her hair into hand, I wrapped it around my wrist and gave it a gentle tug.

"I think, my dear, I should know you in any form."

Then throwing caution to the wind, I kissed her cheek.

We'd already had sex. I could have claimed her lips, made her open her mouth to me, forced her to give me her tongue, get her hot and ready for me so that she'd beg me to explore every inch of her.

But for all that Thalassa was wild and unpredictable, there was an inherent innocence to her as well. I liked every aspect of her personality so far, but the innocence intrigued me most. There were so few things in the world that that could truly be said of.

Her fingers brushed over her cheek like the whisper of butterfly wings.

We, neither of us spoke, simply gazed into each other's eyes. I was drawn to her. And I believed her to be drawn to me as well.

I couldn't understand it, but I liked it.

She vanished seconds later. Simply disappeared. I stood like a fool in that empty doorway for what felt like hours afterward.

This imprisonment wasn't so bad when she was around. But without her, I felt every second of my incarceration.

Chapter 7

Calypso

"Shilling for your thoughts," Nimue said softly.

"Hm?" I glanced up at her with a frown.

She was dressed in a soft gown of spun glowworm silk dyed a rich, brocaded blue. Her dark hair was pinned high on her head, with a simple curl laid across her shoulder. And she held a spoonful of soup inches from her mouth, staring at me as though I'd suddenly sprouted a third eye.

"What?" I made a show of rubbing my palms across my fin.

As she set the spoon down in her half-empty bowl of clam chowder, a pretty frown marred her forehead.

"You'll give yourself wrinkles, mistress," I chastised her, rubbing a thumb across it and smoothing out her skin, which was much too motherly an action for a servant to take.

Good gods, I felt so out of it today.

"I'm sorry," I folded my hands in my lap. "I'm not quite sure what's come over me today."

"Sex, I'd imagine."

Jutting my jaw, I nodded. "Yes, I did have it last night. But why would sex make me feel so discombobulated?"

A servant—a maiden I recognized as Stygia—idled by, peeked in at the two of us, and swiftly turned on her fin, swimming in the other direction.

My murderous glare probably had something to do with her reaction; then again, I'd not quite forgiven Stygia for nearly destroying my children's happiness, not the way Nim and Sircco had.

Those two had such soft, mushy hearts.

"I suppose it is time to talk of the birds and the bees."

"Why? I wish to speak of sex, Consort."

Her sparkling laughter lifted my mood just slightly.

"It is called a euphemism, Janita. A polite way of referencing romance, sex, and what not."

"It is stupid."

She shrugged. "Fine, let's talk about sex in all its glorious detail. Was it debauched, naughty, did you flog that dolphin?"

What in the world was she talking about? I patted her hand, fearing my daughter-in-law was quite out of her mind. "There weren't no dolphins in the room, mistress."

Flinching, looking as though she'd just bitten into a sour lemon, she waved a hand. "Never mind. What I want to know is, how did it go?"

Surely they'd felt the raw currents of power Hades and I had created. Then again, I wasn't supposed to be Calypso right now.

"Fine. We had sex and I loved it. His cock felt lovely. Yes. Lovely." I shook my head, but still a frown tugged at my lips.

As if sensing I was still mulling over my thoughts, Nim said nothing. She resumed eating the chowder I'd made her.

"I do not think our arrangement is going to work out," I said it, looking up at her with a little bit of shock at my own words, but realizing they were also true.

My heart was heavy, because it wouldn't work. It couldn't possibly.

"The sex, you don't wish to have sex with him again? But I thought you said you liked it?"

"Oh, I loved it. I want more, in fact." I blinked, adjusting my fishy bum on the seat. "The problem is he touches me too much."

"Mm. Janita, there is a fair bit of touching involved in the act."

"No," I flicked a wrist, "I can handle that kind of touching. I mean, he kissed my cheek this afternoon and last night, after I'd floated his bottom—"

"Mmhmm." She bit her lip.

"He called me by a name. And it'd sounded an awful lot like a pet name."

It'd felt too familiar, too...nice.

It wasn't that I didn't want what I'd witnessed between Nim and Sircco, but the intimacy of more was rather terrifying now that Hades had opened the door that way.

I was a woman used to having my way, doing as I willed, when I willed it. Men were bothersome bores good for only one thing.

And yet when he'd looked into my eyes today my soul had quivered.

"That all sounds wonderful to me," Nim said.

"Not to me," I shook my head. "I do not want more than sex. I will give him two weeks of sex and then I am sending him away for good."

"Hm." Her eyes clouded and she pretended to busy herself with reaching for the bread basket, but there was hardly anything left but crumbs.

"What, hm?" I crossed my arms, being far more demanding with her than Janita had a right to be, but I was truly concerned. I'd hardly slept last night.

"Only that it's impossible to control the heart, Janita. It wants what it wants. If you don't wish to have him fall for you, then make it clear before things become messy and complicated. If you simply want sex, tell him so."

"I assumed I'd done that last night. I rode him, got off him, and walked away. Surely any man should have gotten the hint."

Her brows lifted high onto her forehead. I wasn't sure why she seemed so shocked by my words.

"What? Did I do wrong?"

"Oh, no." She waved her hands. "Not at all. What you did was probably the epitome of most men's dreams. Sex with no strings. I'd imagine many a man would happily sell his soul for such an arrangement."

Nodding, I threw my hands up. "My point exactly. I find our arrangement to be more than satisfactory."

"But—" she held up a finger.

"But?"

"But not all men are built that way. Some actually do have hearts. I know it's an aberration of nature, but there you have it."

"Are you saying my man has a heart?"

Staring at me thoughtfully, she nodded slowly. "Janita, you are a beautiful, interesting, mysterious, and complicated woman. You will find that most men who come up against you will fall prey to your unwitting charm."

"This is true, I am all those things." I nodded. My Nim was quite wise. "But I don't want more, Consort. Especially not with him. We can't work this out, and I'm in no rush to entangle myself permanently with a male. I rather enjoy me life."

"Sircco makes me happy. I adore him. But I am a free woman, Janita. That hasn't changed. The best part about him is that he lets me be who I am, and I think that is a trademark all good couples share. Your mystery man may or may not be a permanent partner in life, but if he is, don't fear where things might lead. You might find life to be twice as interesting with him in it as without him."

I'd had sex with Hades only once. Last night could well have been a fluke. I'd wanted a partner, and he'd filled a role. Tonight would be different. I'd shield any emotion from him.

I'd give him whatever he asked, within reason of course, and explain to him gently that there would be nothing more from me than my body.

He'd be happy.

"Thank you, Consort. I know what I must do now." Getting up, I made as though to leave, but she held me back with a hand to my elbow.

"Be aware of one thing, my dear. The giving of our bodies, while pleasurable, comes with a cost."

I frowned. I'd never heard of such a thing. "Does he wish money for his body?"

She laughed. "Not unless he's in that profession." But her laughter turned quickly serious and her visage thoughtful. "You are a virgin, or were, and the first time leaves a lasting impression, good, bad, or otherwise. We always remember our first. And sometimes our first can haunt us for eternity. If you do not wish to lose your heart to him, guard it well, and consider cutting ties sooner rather than later."

Releasing me, she nodded.

I felt shaken to my very core. I'd never even considered that a possibility. I was a goddess, though; that was only mortal emotion she spoke of. I was above such trials, surely.

Rubbing my arms, I made for home, but rather than rush to him as I had yesterday, I took my time, meandering through Seren until the light had vanished from the waters and they were a heavy navy blue and twinkling from the glow of silver fish.

Hades

I was in a foul mood. She'd abandoned me to this room for hours. I'd tried at one point to head to the kitchens for some food but found I could not step foot outside the door.

Calypso had enchanted the waters.

She also had no staff. Why did a goddess have no staff?

Gnashing my teeth, I sat on the edge of the bed, ready to confess my sins and go, when the waters swirled with pink.

"Aphrodite," I sighed the moment she materialized before me.

Smiling broadly, she sat beside me on the bed, crossed her legs, and glanced around.

"Nice digs."

I shrugged.

"So." She slapped her hands to her knees, causing her breasts to bounce perkily. "I came to give you the daily update."

"Yes?" I asked, bored already.

I knew what was coming. It was only a matter of time before they discovered the truth for themselves.

"Cerberus has been found." She clapped her hands, giving me a broad smile. "I figured you'd like to know your feral monster is now safe and sound and back guarding Tartarus's gates where he belongs."

I was pleased to hear my beast was back.

"Thank you."

Tipping her head, she peered up at me like a barnyard owl. "You don't sound all that happy, H-man, what gives?"

"Nothing," I couldn't quite hide the grumbling tone. "Only that I'm stuck in this hellhole, I couldn't even take a piss today, and I've eaten nothing since this morning."

Aphrodite chuckled. "Calypso takes being your warden seriously, obviously."

In truth, I wasn't even that hungry or needing to use the restroom. But I was bored out of my skull.

"So how'd the bow chicka wow wow go?" Her smile was broad.

"Sensed that, did you?" I snorted.

"You kidding, we all felt the aftershocks of that wave like a freaking earthquake. You kids are so much fun to watch."

I twirled on her. "You'd better not be spying on us, Dite, or I'll kick you into the Styx and never let you leave."

Sticking out her tongue, she tapped her chest. "Give me some credit, here, kay. I don't need to spy. But like I said, you guys weren't exactly inconspicuous either. Jeez. By the by," she airily switched subjects, "Apollo wanted me to tell your girl he's super pissed, and if she shows her face in the Above sometime before the next two weeks are out, he'll scorch her ass. His words, not mine."

I felt my face contort, felt the bone sculpt out further, turning me from flesh to Death in an instant. "He lays a hand on her and he'll live to regret it."

Looking taken aback by my obvious vehemence, she held up her hands. "Dude, take it down a notch. I'm just the messenger. And holy crap, you've got it bad. Little bit of tail and you're lost on her. Good grief."

Running fingers through my hair, I flicked a hand through her image, banishing her with a touch.

"No, I'm not," I whispered to no one.

A minute later, Calypso appeared.

A woman of water and form, her movements so sensuous, so alluring that I knew my words for the lie they were. I was losing myself to her, and I hated myself for it.

Chapter 8

Calypso

I'd heard him. Heard the conversation he'd had with Dite. And even as I breathed a sigh of relief, a knot formed in my stomach. How dare he not be lost on me!

"You are not lost on me." I laughed and flattened my palms on my hips, rocking on my heels in a pose I'd once seen a prostitute use in a whorehouse. I had one knee tipped just slightly forward, with my legs spread wide and my body on full view for him.

I smirked when Hades shook his head like a man who'd just been blinded by the sun.

"I'll make you so lost on me, you foul man. Now get on your knees and beg." I pointed to the ground.

I wasn't really sure why some women said that, but I'd heard it often enough to believe it held some merit.

But Hades, as bespelled by me as he was, was no mere mortal. Crossing his impressive arms over his equally impressive chest, he snapped his fingers, and because I'd given him my oath last night to do as he bid, my own enchantments worked against me.

Instead of me being the one commanding him to obedience, I was the one now locked and chained to the bed with my legs spread wide to the world. Although my cuffs were furry and pink.

"Well," I grumped, shaking my wrists a little, "so this is what it feels like. Now you may release me, male."

His grin made my heart stutter. He was truly fun to look at. And suddenly all my fears of the past few hours melted away under the excitement of our bed games.

"If you'll remember, Calypso, you promised me every other night. This is my night, and I will take my due."

When I'd left him this morning, he'd been casually dressed. But at some point he'd changed, because he was now undoing his tie, and just that small movement made me want to pant as he casually revealed a small sliver of his swarthy flesh one tantalizing and agonizing inch at time.

"I find myself cross with you today, Thalassa."

I was like a dogfish in heat. I arched against the bonds, but really, I was rather intrigued by what he'd planned for me.

"Oh, I know this game." Clearing my throat, I whispered meekly, "Yes, Master."

He arched a devilish brow. Long, blunt fingers undid the first three buttons of his black silk shirt.

"You will only address me as Master from here on out. Do you understand me?"

"Yes, Master," I gulped, still sort of straining against the furry cuffs. I wet my lips when he finally slid the shirt off, revealing all that yummy ropey muscle.

His skin was so tight, his muscles rigid and powerful looking. Even covered in the scars, I was sure I'd never seen a man half as glorious as he.

"I want to lick you," I murmured dreamily.

To which he reared his hand back and swatted the side of my ass. Yipping, I half jumped off the bed, dragged down only because of the cuffs.

"You bastard!" I hissed, ready to drive a spear through his gut for the outrage.

Lifting a hand again, he cocked his brow. "Remember your manners, Thalassa. For tonight, I am your master."

Oh, the game. Bloody hell.

"Yes, Master," I grumped, and then wiggled my foot. "My thigh burns, you a-hole."

Sitting on the edge of the bed, he gently ran his callused palm across the place he'd smacked, and I had to admit, it felt dreamy.

Whimpering in the back of my throat, I tried to wiggle into his touch a little deeper, wanting to feel his weight already and flog his dolphin with my blowhole.

Obsidian eyes gleamed as though he knew my thoughts. He probably did; I wasn't trying to hide my lust for him.

Clearing his throat, he stood back up, and I felt bereft of his touch. I was addicted to the feel of this man.

His hands landed on his pants, but instead of undoing them, he merely rested his fingers and looked at me. I was ready to yell at him to take it off already.

"Do you want to know why I'm cross with you, Thalassa?"

I rolled my eyes. "Not really, Master. And I do wish you'd stop calling me Thalassa. You make me want to retch when you do that. Also, are you going to pound me yet or what?"

Walking over to the vanity, he rested his weight against it and gave me an amused look. "You're a horrible slave."

"And you're a terrible master. What's a girl got to do to get laid around here?" I jerked my hips upward, spreading my legs just a little more so that he'd take a good, hard look at the evidence of my desire.

He gulped but quickly shook his head.

"I'm hungry. And I haven't used the restroom the entire day."

Oops.

Well, that put a damper on things.

"You're a god. You don't have to take a dump, Master."

"That's besides the point, Thalassa."

I mock gagged.

"Stop."

"You stop."

He growled. And it was so cute I couldn't help but chuckle.

"I can get out of these cuffs if I really want to."

"Yes, I'd imagine you could. Revoke your word, and you can do as you please." He shrugged, seeming entirely too unconcerned for my peace of mind.

I narrowed my eyes. "Do you not wish to bed me anymore, Hades?"

He pursed his lips.

It'd only been one day. Had I done it wrong that he held me chained? At least I'd put him out of his misery quickly.

Pointing at his pants, he muttered, "You can see that I do."

I grinned, licking my lips. I wondered what he would taste like. Oh, that would go on my list of things to do.

"Then what's the problem?"

"I'm hungry."

"No, you're not."

"Damn it, woman, no I'm not. But you cannot leave me to rot in this cell for the entire day without something to entertain myself with. Do you hear me?"

He genuinely sounded grumpy about it. "Would it make you feel any better if I said I just forgot?"

His deep voice rolled across my skin like sun-warmed honey. "What do you think?"

"I'm guessing not."

Hades shook his head, causing some of his hair to spill across his forehead. He was generally neat in appearance; immaculate would be the proper word.

Seeing him so casual in such an intimate setting had me thinking crazy, wicked thoughts. Thoughts like never letting him out of this room again for the rest of eternity.

"Master," I said it softly.

His nostrils flared. The man looked like a devil, and he made my soul dance.

"Speak, slave."

"I have an ouch right here." I thrust my hips up.

"Do you?" A wicked glint filled his eyes.

"Yes."

His fingers stroked the vanity the way I wished they'd start stroking me. He had such beautiful hands, big and veiny. I wanted them all over me right now.

"And what do you think I should do about that, slave?"

"Kiss it better," I chirped.

I'd expected him to say no, or at the very least to say I was a bad girl who did not deserve her master's favor. He did neither.

Hades was on me in a flash, covering my body with his own like a living blanket but careful to keep his weight on his arms.

"Say that again, slave," he demanded, and goddess, I obeyed.

"Kiss me better," I breathed like a lusty little kitten.

With a hungry groan, he tore at my lips. He was wild, and I loved it. I melted against him.

I wanted to touch him, touch every square inch of him, but I was still bound.

"Release me," I demanded.

"No," he snarled, then nipped at my jaw. The bite was hard, brutal, and excited me to my very core.

My blood sang, and I grew dizzy with lust.

Then his tongue was dancing along my flesh where he'd bitten, and all I could do was grunt my pleasure, shoving myself upward as best I could, trying to create some sort of friction against the bulge in his pants.

"Don't move, or I'll stop," he snapped with eyes blazing like cut jewels.

Feeling both strangely lethargic and flat-out lusty as hell, I would have handed him my soul just then if he'd demanded it.

"Yes, Master."

A rumble exploded from his chest. The man was turning into a beast before my very eyes. The depths of his passions electrified me, spurred on my own.

I didn't move, but I couldn't help that the waters swirled, that a tempest raged outside these walls. My powers were out of my control for the moment.

He moved down my body, nipping and laving with his tongue along the way, circling first one nipple and then the other. His hands were squeezing my hips, and I tingled everywhere.

I was nothing but a bundle of excited nerves.

Hades was at my navel, then below it, then right at the line of my pubis. I practically drooled on myself, knowing what came next. I'd never had anyone touch me there save for him. Many times I'd watched mortals exploring each other's bodies in the dead of night, and always one thing seemed to bring out the animal in them more than anything else: the touching of tongues to the jewels of the body.

Vertigo held me fast, I was ready to be swept up by the tide of his devotion, when suddenly it all stopped.

His weight was gone, and I was cold.

Opening my eyes, it took my dazed mind a second to realize he was standing back where he'd been before and gazing at me with a cocky grin.

"You bastard! Get back here," I barked, ready to rip his balls off his body if he didn't return to me at once and pleasure me.

He shrugged. "I'm hungry, Thalassa. I've not yet been fed, and I find my energies flagging."

My nostrils flared. "You want food. Fine."

With a snap of fingers, I dropped heaping platters of whatever I could think of down onto the vanity. The room dripped with scents of roasted meat, brined olives, sweet pomegranates, and herb-scented rices.

"Thank you." He grinned. Then, turning his back to me, he sat and began eating.

Surely he was kidding. Trying to get at me. But as the minutes ticked by with no hint of him stopping, I finally lost my head.

"I hate you!"

"No, you don't." He winked at me in the mirror.

If I revoked my word, he won. He was practically daring me to do it.

"I do, I hate you all."

"Let's not pretend with one another, my dear. It is beneath us both." Turning, he dabbed at his mouth with a napkin, all calm, cool, and collected as could be.

I'd seen the beast and now I was seeing the gentleman, and they both drove me mad.

Sighing, I calmed the waters and tried to relax. He wanted to wait me out. Well, two could play this game.

"How's the food?"

"Delicious." He inclined his head, taking a sip from a golden goblet full of ambrosia.

"I want some."

"No." He tilted his brow. "I've got other plans for you tonight."

"And just when do you *plan* to do me, Dead Boy?"

"When I'm ready." He crossed his leg.

He wore no shirt, just silk trousers with black loafers. He should look a fool. He did not.

Again he was staring me down, devouring me with his steely eyes. And the room was fraught with tension so thick I could hardly breathe around it.

My ears started buzzing; my body trembled. It was hard to remember to stay in form. I felt exposed, and not just physically. I didn't care about being naked in front of him. It was my natural state after all. But Hades wasn't just studying me, he was memorizing me. Every line, every curve. His gaze slowly consumed me.

I'd been annoyed with him, and now I could hardly remember my name.

Standing, he walked slowly back to my side once more. Never once saying a word, he released me from my bonds. I felt suddenly unsure without them.

It was such a strange, vulnerable feeling, not knowing what he meant to do to me.

Planting his hands on my hips, he turned me so that now my legs dangled over the edge of the bed.

Fire danced through his eyes as he stared boldly at my center.

I swallowed hard when he dropped to his knees and, without saying a word, took me into his mouth.

I bucked, and a groan that sounded almost like pain rumbled from my chest. Instinctively, I wrapped my legs around his shoulders and writhed, dancing on his mouth as his tongue skated across my center.

His touch was like a shock of lightning. I couldn't believe or understand what was happening to me, the raw tempest of desire obliterating every rational thought in my head. I was a creature of one need.

Desire.

Clawing at the back of his head, I whimpered, pleading in gibberish for him to end this agony.

But Hades was not to be rushed. His timing didn't alter. His movements were precise and purposeful, drawing me in deeper and deeper, making me feel like I'd been snared within the folds of a spider's web.

Spots danced before my eyes, and blackness threatened to take me under.

"It wasn't supposed to be like this," I vaguely heard myself mutter. I wasn't even sure why I'd said that. But I couldn't seem to stop the deluge from pouring out. "Oh, Hades. Oh, my Darkness."

And then I was there, cresting that pinnacle that literally fractured my body into a million prisms of bliss. I could no longer contain my form. I needed to be free, needed to be all. If I hadn't left this body, I wouldn't have survived the taking.

My soul slipped free, and I was me again. I was the Sea, I was all things. I wrapped myself around his body, anchoring myself as best as I could as my waters continued to churn with pleasure so intense it was nearly a knifing pain.

Life exploded from within me. Creatures swam up from the deep. My children came out to greet me, to comfort me, but I couldn't stop myself from floating away. I couldn't think clearly.

Hades, I whispered on a current, *save me...*

And I felt him. Felt him take me in. Hold me fast.

I clung to him, trembling in his arms, but his grip was unyielding, demanding.

"Look into my eyes, Thalassa," he commanded.

I did. And finally I felt the fury of this taking begin to release me, I was steadied, calmed.

And I was terrified by the power I'd just given him over me.

With a cry, I rushed from his arms, losing myself in the deep, far, far away from him and his paralyzing, magical touch.

"I just need a moment to compose myself. Just a minute."

But as I knelt there shivering, I knew those words were little more than a big, fat lie.

Chapter 9

Hades

She left me.

And I stumbled backward onto the bed, rocked by the intensity of my own emotions.

The seas burbled with life, glowing with the colors of creatures familiar and bizarre as they buzzed through the waters searching out their queen. Fins brushed by me, an array of fish swirling like glinting steel.

I wasn't bothered by the crush of them. Not even by the long-tailed serpents that slithered between my legs.

These animals had been born the moment she'd shattered in my arms. I'd never experienced something so...profound in all my life. And the taste of her, it was magic.

Looking at the door, I could tell she'd dropped the enchantment. I was free to move unmolested through her halls, but I found I had no desire to leave this room.

The halls of my temple were always full to bursting with the dead seeking me out, needing my ear to settle matters. I'd not known a moment's peace in all my days.

Wetting my lips, I imagined what I would do, where I would go if I were her. Something had passed between us this night, something neither of us had been prepared for.

She'd created life under my touch.

I'd been with goddesses and mortals, and sex was always just sex. I'd felt my own powers manifest with my first taste of her, felt the fires of death rage through my blood, fill my eyes. If she'd been a human, she'd have been consumed, her lifeline cut short.

But Calypso had taken all I'd had to give and turned my curse into a blessing.

I stared without seeing at the door for what must have been an hour, trying to make sense of what my life had now become. But answers eluded me. The animals were long gone.

Standing, feeling the need to pace, I walked back and forth for a moment until a strange blue glow attracted me to the window.

It was her.

Nothing now but a towering, watery pillar of femininity, she walked with the casual grace of the newly dead. What I'd assumed to be a gown made of diamonds covering her from her neck to her toes was actually a small school of silvery fish.

Green hair undulated behind her in the gentle waves. Wherever she stepped, green sea moss grew, carpeting the sands beneath her feet. Swimming idly behind her was a massive great white shark.

She reminded me of a ghost, of the newly dead who came to my halls, moving as though with the grace of life still kissing their souls, untouchable and unbearably beautiful to behold.

I palmed my chest over the spot of my furiously beating heart, telling myself that this was nothing. What we had was idle play, what all Olympians did when needing to satisfy the lusts of the flesh. None of us truly cared for each other. Not in the way I saw my dead care.

The dead had always appealed to me. They were more real than the petty, selfish, creatures I called "family." Humans had a way of truly understanding and appreciating the value of another. There was a lot of ugliness in their world, but there was also more laughter, more verve, and more truth among them.

Calypso, having not lived among any of us, was her own being. She did not understand our politics, nor did she care to learn them. She'd offered to take me in because she'd wanted me. Selfish, possibly, but also honest.

She wanted nothing more from me than what I wasn't already willing to give. In many ways she was like my dead, the very best parts of them.

"Thalassa," I whispered.

And even though we were separated by thick walls of coral and rock, she stopped walking. Her spine went straight and stiff, and her head turned just slightly to the side, giving me her profile.

"I know what happened to her," I said. "They will find me guilty."

Her fingers twitched by her side.

My heart was heavy, my stomach sick with nerves. I wouldn't die from the tortures, but it would be far from pleasant.

Did you kill her?

Her words filled my head, and I shook it. "No. I did not. But I know where she is now."

I thought she would ask me where, but she didn't.

Tell me no more, Hades.

I frowned.

As though sensing my confusion, she shook her head. *The waters are not ours alone tonight. I sense Poseidon's cronies listening in.*

Clenching my jaw, I went to move back to my bed, but she turned and locked eyes with me.

They glowed just like the rest of her. Goddess, she was breathtaking. I'd not noticed the bright-pink sea rose she'd tucked into her hair, but now that I did, I couldn't help but smile.

So ancient, and yet so youthful in so many ways.

Take your rest now. I will keep you safe.

Only with her did that statement not feel ridiculous. Unspoken were the words that soon I'd be convicted and would know no peace for a millennia. But I was far from tired. My mind could not stop working.

Hades?

"Yes?"

She didn't fidget, but I could sense her reticence.

Would you like to come to work with me tomorrow?

"You work?" I couldn't quite hide my shock. Looking her up and down, dressed as the regal goddess she truly was, I suddenly recalled the tantalizing Janita in her servant's clothes.

Her laughter bubbled through my dark soul.

I find I rather have a knack for it.

More curious than I had a right to be, I nodded. "I would be honored."

Her lips pressed down tight, and she looked so innocent. I knew the vixen she was, but now I was getting to see an entirely different side to her.

"'A many-faceted temptress,'" I murmured, "'her depths unknowable, her passions tempestuous, and with one kiss, a man's ruin...'"

Many poems had been written about the sea. That had always been one of my favorites, and the words now seemed truer than ever.

Lifting her chin high, she gave me a regal curtsy, then turned and slowly walked away.

Calypso

Why in Tartarus had I offered to take him with me this morning?

Grumpy, I knotted the sash of my servant's apron around my trim tail.

Linx snuffled.

"What?" I snapped.

You know what.

"No, Linx," I looked at her cross-eyed, "I'm sure that I don't."

I know she knew what I was feeling; we were two halves of the same whole, after all. But I refused to acknowledge that I was a foul, temperamental hagfish this morning. That currently the seas were rocking violently and that pirates and sailors alike were eyeing the horizon with wary, fearful eyes. I was at the point that if I even broke a nail, I'd probably pitch a fit and sink at least ten vessels, just for the hell of it.

Huffing, feeling her censure like a heavy brand, I flicked my tail, causing the ground beneath to rumble and the fault lines to groan.

"Fine. You want to know what my problem is, I'll tell you. My problem is the fact that when I'm not with Hades, my mind is clear, focused. I know what I must do. Have sex. Have fun. And then send him on his merry way once I'm through."

But then I thought about his eyes last night, so haunted, so open to me, and my traitorous heart had trembled at the sight of it. I'd wanted to hold him. To rock him to my breast. And not for sex at all. But to hold him.

Hold him!

I tapped my breast. "I am a goddess. I am not to be chained down. I am not to feel these trivial, sentimental, mawkish—"

Calypso, she warned, *you're doing it again.*

"What?" I frowned, and then realized in an instant that the furniture in the room was shaking violently from a swift, rolling current.

Blowing out a heavy breath, I pinched the bridge of my nose. If I didn't watch it, I'd kill all my children. The only things precious to me in this world were them, and some (I thought of Nim) more than others.

"Bloody poop, I'm in a foul mood."

Linx wrinkled her nose.

Why did you offer to take him with you to the castle today, then?

Plopping my fishy butt down on the clam-shell bed, I planted my chin on my fist and stared broodily at my sister.

She was so pretty. Why couldn't I have been born her instead of me? Instead of this volatile, emotive crazy woman who could hardly make sense of her own emotions half the time.

"I wish I were you," I murmured. "Do you not suffer from loneliness ever, my Linx?"

Shaking her equine head, she delicately nibbled on a mound of crab apples.

I have you. I need nothing else. But you were never like me, Caly, and that is okay. You are you, and I adore you for who you are.

I curled my lip. "I am a scatterbrained nitwit. I offered to take Hades with me last night because I missed him. Can you imagine? He'd just given me pleasure, and I was satisfied. Why was that not enough? Suddenly I miss him and want to be where he is and wonder what clothes he wears today and whether I can taste his cock as he tasted my pearl and—"

Linx's laughter flitted through my head like sea bells. *Seems to me you've developed quite an attachment to him.*

"Yes, but I didn't want to!" I knew I was acting petulant, but I neither cared nor desired to act adult at the moment. There were some days when being a grown-up sucked. Today was one of them.

My heart ached. Literally ached in my chest. And how was that possible? Why had sleeping with him made me feel all these violent, maudlin emotions?

Hades was a horrible man. He'd schemed to keep Persephone by tricking her with his pomegranates, and he'd basically admitted to me to having done something nefarious to her. He was known to be rude, dismissive, cold, and calculating.

Of course, the last few qualities I found rather charming, as I, too, had my moments.

Stupid, perfidious heart. I couldn't even list his flaws without wanting to defend them, even if only to myself.

Gnashing my teeth, I glowered at my sister. "I like him."

The words were ripped from me.

Yes, I know, love, it's quite obvious. She slurped down an apple that'd tried to wiggle away. I frowned. Apples didn't wiggle, and then I realized a couple of hermit crabs had hidden themselves in with the batch of apples.

I had to swallow my gag. Linx and I were both vegetarians. I found the thought of eating my own a little on the cannibalistic side. If she knew what she'd done, she would vomit, and I would have a major mess on my hands. Hippocampus vom was far from pleasant; it smelled a little like horse dung and looked like putrid soup. But...as she hadn't seemed to notice, I wouldn't tell her.

Getting up, I pretended to swim toward my vanity but instead accidentally on purpose flicked my tail at her bowl, causing the other hermits to scatter out and disappear.

Linx blew out an agitated breath. She knew I'd done it on purpose. She didn't know why.

Caly.

"Linxy." I rolled my eyes and patted my silvery hair back into place. I looked so sexy this morning. There was a flush to my cheeks, and my thick hair was caught up in a plait that danged like a horse's tail across my bare shoulder.

I'd worn one of my prettier outfits, really just strategically placed pearls of differing lengths wrapped around me, so that each time I moved it highlighted my sensual curves.

While I didn't exactly look ready to go cook and clean, I was beautiful. And that counted for far more.

My stomach dived. "I fear I have developed an infatuation with the beast, my darling."

Infatuations end, Calypso. Linx spoke as she nudged the last apple back into her bowl with the tip of her nose. *Ride this out, and I'm sure you'll be back to your old self in no time. Have sex. Make babies. Have fun. And for the love of Rhea, stop overthinking everything so much.*

"It's not exactly overthinking. Do you know he killed Persephone?"

Beautiful, horsy eyes widened. *He did? I thought you said it wasn't—*

I flicked my wrist. "Well, I'm not sure he killed her, but he knows what happened to her. They'll come for him, no doubt. They'll take him from me."

You sound displeased by that.

There were no words for me to say to that. But they stayed with me throughout the rest of the day.

Chapter 10

Hades

I'd been to Zeus's temple, the palace in the clouds, the crown jewel of all of Olympus. A shining, majestic place crafted of the finest white marble, nestled upon a fluffy bank of clouds thicker than a marshmallow topping, where sunlight never faded and wine flowed freely.

My own Elysian fields were another wonder, a verdant Eden of blooms and greenery, where the faithful frolicked and reveled throughout all eternity.

Demeter's vast fields of wheat.

Dite's love temple dripping with the sensuous fragrances of myrrh and nubile, ripe women who lived only to worship their mistress.

All of them beautiful, but none of them quite as enchanting to me as the sea garden Nimue—King Consort— and Calypso took me too.

It was an underwater oasis, rolling green hills surrounded by jeweled strands of blue and green kelp that grew up from the ocean floor, where tiny and colorful fish swam through. A waterfall cascaded from the cliff face of a massive mountain range several yards before us.

Bird fish flew through the azure, tropical waters, singing as they dived for their own meals.

I rested my weight against an alabaster rock poking up from the ground, simply watching them.

Nimue was pale with dark hair and eyes. She was ripe with child, her figure lush and enticing. But she paled in comparison to the maiden fussing beside her.

My enchantress was yet again in Janita form, though today she'd broadened her hips just slightly, making an already delectable rear positively mouthwatering. Her breasts had likewise grown in mass, so that if I palmed them, I could not cup them entirely.

Calypso had failed to introduce me to Nimue, so the Consort had had to do it on her own. But I could tell many things from studying them now.

The first was that Nimue was of far greater significance to Calypso than she'd initially let on. The second was that though Calypso disguised herself, Nimue knew who she really was, though the goddess herself seemed completely unaware of that fact.

"Tut tut, ye sit here, now, out of the burning sun," Caly murmured tenderly, pointing at a spot on the blanket she'd tucked beneath a large overhang of rock so that, indeed, Nimue would be out of the noonday sun that wasn't really sun at all.

"Janita, honestly, I'm fin—"

"Sit." Calypso brooked no argument, pushing the Consort down with a firm shove.

The consort dropped, casting me a grumpy frown that soon turned into an exasperated sort of forbearance.

"As you wish, Janita. Though I really do wish you'd stop fussing over me. I'm a woman."

"Ye're naught but a child." Janita fluffed up the consort's skirts. Then, with a final gentle pat to her knee, she turned and headed toward the basket of foods she'd left packed in the carriage some yards back.

"Come here," Nimue commanded to me when Janita had moved off.

Grinning at being commanded so, I decided to oblige her. The woman was precious to Calypso, so I could do no less.

Taking a seat on the opposite corner, I nocked a knee and inclined my head. "Consort, how may I serve?"

Her eyes were wise, intelligent. This was a woman who missed nothing. Tapping her temple, she shot out a brief thought.

You can hear me, can't you?

My lips curled at the edges. *Yes.*

Good. Then tell me, who are you really? I know you are her sex partner, but you are no mere legger.

Lifting a brow, I debated whether to answer. I had no need to answer her. She was no authority to me. But I rather liked the pretty little human. I hardly knew her, but she intrigued me nonetheless, so I decided to be honest with her.

I am Hades.

She blinked twice, swallowed, and then patted her chest. *As in the—*

Yes.

Shock flitted through her gaze as she glanced back at the carriage and then darted her eyes back to me. *Goddess, Calypso sure knows how to pick 'em.*

My lips twitched, and I dipped my head, taking it as a compliment, whether it was intended to be or not.

Well, I was going to threaten to cut your balls off if you hurt her, but I rather think that would be impossible with you.

Chuckling beneath my breath, I could see where Calypso had adopted her strange idioms. *There is no need to worry about me, Consort. I leave in a matter of days.*

Where are you going? Her fingers toyed with the petals of a baby sea bell, causing gold dust to scatter through the waters.

Hell, more likely.

Bow-shaped lips pursed. *Hades, are you to bring war to my mate's kingdom? Tell me now.*

Touching a fist to my heart, I shook my head. *I vow to do no such. I am here only temporarily and only on the queen's mercy.*

Do you like her?

It seemed to me there was a wealth of meaning hidden behind the simple words.

I shrugged. *We hardly know one another.*

She shook her head and then cleared her throat.

The next moment, I spied Calypso, with an armful of goods, bending over, giving me a tantalizing glimpse of her round posterior, and I couldn't help but snort. The woman was maddening even when she didn't try to be.

Humming softly beneath her breath, she set her baskets down, lifted the lid, and began pulling out bottles of wine, roasts of fowl, bowls of creamy cheeses, nuts, olives, loaves of bread, and on and on and on it went, food for as far as the eye could see.

"Oh damn," she frowned, "I forgot the caviar, and I know how fond of that ye are, Consort."

"Janita, please, this spread would feed an army. There is no need—"

"Pft!" Janita raspberried cutely, shushing Nimue with a heavy shake of her head, causing the delicate pearls around her breasts to bob and sway, forcing my eyes (as though by magic; fancy that) to gravitate to her pointed, coral-colored nipples. "None of that, now. I promised ye a feast, and a feast I'll deliver. One moment."

With a happy grin, she swam off.

This was a side of the goddess I'd never seen. Nurturing mother.

And that's when it hit me: Nimue was none other than the wife of Calypso's son, Sircco.

Something decidedly warm spread through my chest. In all my days, I'd never once seen Persephone so doting. Not to me, not to another male, not even to an animal. The self-centered whelp had only cared for herself.

I felt Nimue's eyes on me. Turning to her, I noticed a shrewd, calculating look.

You do like her, whether you wish to acknowledge it or not.

I shrugged. No sense in denying it. No sense in adding to it, either.

If there is one thing I know about my mother-in-law, Hades, it is this: When she falls, she falls hard, and her love, while exceedingly rare, is a gift to be handled with the greatest reverence. She is a treasure worth savoring. Treat her well, and there is nothing that should be impossible to you.

I pondered her words. I was a god. There was nothing impossible to me. And yet I could not change my fate. I'd had a hand in Persephone's disappearance. My destiny was sealed and in the hands of a blind justice.

Janita laughed. "I've got it!" She held up a tin of Beluga caviar the size of her head. "I knew I'd packed this beast away somewheres. Now," she swam to our side, dropping to the other side of me and setting the tin down. "Let's get our chow on."

Calypso

"Ladies, I need to use the necessaries." Hades' thick voice—like sun-warmed molasses—rolled over me and made me shiver.

I didn't look at him when he got up, bowed to Nim, and sauntered off into the brush. I'd told him to act human, and taking a piss was about as human as it came, I supposed.

"I like him," Nimue said without preamble once he was out of hearing range. "What's his name, Janita? You never have said."

Thinking on the fly, I latched onto the first name I thought of. "Harvey."

"Harvey. Odd name." She delicately nibbled on a cracker that held a heaping dollop of caviar.

"Mmhmm." I pretended to fluff at a loose sliver of hair, which did not in fact exist, as I was perfectly coifed today.

"Such manners he has. That voice," she smirked, "and that body."

A fierce heat rose to my cheeks. "Yes," I sighed, "he does have a banging one. His stomach is shredded and his thighs like redwoods and his arms...Oh, goddess," I fluttered my lashes, remembering the way he'd held all that glorious weight up on his arms as he'd tasted and suckled at my breasts. "He is lovely. He is also covered in scars."

"Scars," she said, frowning softly.

I smoothed out the line between her brows by reflex.

"Oh, yes," I continued, "from here," I pointed to the hollow of my throat, "to here," I trailed my finger down to my pubis.

"Why?" she asked as she swallowed her last bite of cracker and then reclined with a heavy sigh. "Gods, Janita, I feel like a whale, but it was wonderful."

Accepting her adulation with a nod, I shrugged. "I do not ken, but I wish I did. I find it exceedingly odd for a man like him to be covered as he is. It smacks of deliberation. Though, I do find the marks to be rather fetching. I oftentimes want to lick my way across each one of 'em."

"You don't say."

"Mmhm. Yes." I popped a sweet sea grape into my mouth, chewing thoughtfully.

Hades was giving us time to talk. I could tell because he was gone far longer than a man should piss.

My realm was beautiful, and it wasn't often I granted my peers permission to access it. I wondered what he thought of it. I'd very much like to explore his Elysian fields someday, perhaps even Tartarus. I was rather fond of fire.

"Ask him."

"What?" I shook my head, scattering the images of ghostly wails and licking flames from my mind's eye. "But why?"

She shrugged. "It's what people generally do when they wish to know one another better."

"But I don't want to know him better, do I?" Why had that popped out a question? I shouldn't want to know him better, and yet it seemed to me that I might actually be lying to myself. I was curious. Far more than I should be.

I also wanted to know what he'd done to Sephone and why. Not that I much cared for that brat, but he couldn't just go off and kill a goddess willy nilly, whether she deserved it or not.

It was god etiquette 101.

After what the pantheon had done to the Titans, the three Fates had decreed no more killing or enslaving of family; otherwise the offender's term as a reigning god would come to a screeching and violent end.

Of course, I was immune to such laws, as I was a Primordial and had had nothing to do with that distasteful uprising. Stupid Psycho, however, was not immune. We might share waters, but I was older than the bastard and twice as powerful, and he knew it. Prick.

Just thinking about Fish Butt made me feel ragey.

"Do you?"

It took me a moment to realize what she was asking. I'd gone off on a tangent again. I was prone to doing that sometimes.

"I shouldn't. He's leaving in a few days."

"That's not an answer, Janita. Even if he leaves, there's nothing saying he couldn't come back."

"Oh no, he's never coming back." I shook my head and then realized she had no idea Harvey was Hades, and I didn't wish to open that can of nematodes at the moment. "What I mean to say is, I very highly doubt he'd be able to return. This is strictly an afternoon-delight type of situation, Consort."

"Well," she plucked up a star bell and began plucking at its petals, "I'm not really sure he sees it that way."

"Really?" I leaned in, heart thumping terribly fast. "Did he tell you something? What did he say?"

She smiled. "Oh, nothing he said with his mouth, but his eyes speak volumes. My mother once told me eyes are the windows to the soul. You see, a man can say anything he wants with his lips, but his eyes always give him away. Look at them next time, and you might just see what I have."

His eyes were lovely. I could drown in their dark pools. But a window? Hm, I would need time to ponder that notion.

"Nimue, he may have done something bad." It was as close as I was willing to come to revealing who he was. I chewed on my bottom lip, not really sure what to expect her to say.

Her shrug spoke volumes. "Yes, but how bad is bad, really? You must remember who my own father is. There are those who'd call him rotten to the core, but I never really saw him that way. Still don't. He is a pirate. It is in his nature to steal, plunder, and loot, but where it matters, his heart is pure."

"See," I pointed at my chest, "I feel the same way. What's a little death now and then, aye?"

Her smile slipped for a millisecond, but then she quickly recovered and laughed. "This is why I like you, Janita. You never fail to shock and amaze."

"Glad I can be of service to you, my dear."

Chapter 11

Calypso

Nimue had to return to the palace soon after. I'd whispered instructions into the ears of the dolphins guiding her chariot to return home promptly upon pain of death should aught happen to her. My grandpups were to be born soon, and none were to harass Nim.

Then with a wave, I'd said my goodbyes. Returning to the blanket, I vanished the nearly empty trays of food and blanket with a flick of my wrist.

"That is a very handy bit of magic, Janita." Hades' words were a rumble in my ear.

And I could not contain the shivers that wracked me at the sound of them. With a curl of my lip, I twirled, swirling my broad, silvery fins around his leg and dragging him closer to me.

"I'm so horny," I whispered, clawing at his shirt.

He looked so yummy today with his black on black on black. I really needed to switch up that man's wardrobe.

And when he grazed my cheek with his knuckles, I saw what Nim had been talking about: the fiery glint in his eyes when he looked at me. The kind of look that stripped away pretense and revealed the raw, unvarnished truths beneath.

"Do you like me, Dead Boy?"

He paused in his touch, and I drowned in his gaze. In my maiden form, we were eye level, but I felt so much smaller. It still scared me, but right now, it was also exhilarating.

"Very much."

His words were a dart that pricked my heart like Cupid's arrow.

"Why did you abandon us for so long?" As we talked, I'd slipped his shirt out of his pants and slid my hands up his warm chest, flicking at the suddenly tight nubs of his nipples.

He bit his bottom lip.

"I sensed your need to talk with your daughter."

I gasped. "You know she's my daughter?"

His smile was tender. Hades didn't say another word; instead he leaned over to kiss me.

And the touch of him was a brand that seared. I parted my lips on a sigh and dueled with his tongue.

We kissed for what felt like an eternity. His cock wedged tight against my tail, and I couldn't help but wiggle on him.

Tails were such incredibly sensitive parts of a maiden's anatomy, far more so than legs. Every molecule of me tingled and ached.

With a thought, I commanded everyone and everything to keep their distance from us. I aimed to keep him entirely to myself this afternoon.

After minutes of sharing breaths and kisses, he finally came up. "Thank you for taking me out of that prison."

"Is my home really a prison to you?"

Hades had thick calluses on his palms. I leaned into them as he framed my face. "Only when you're absent."

"Do you wish to sex me, Dead Boy?"

"Gods yes," he growled and I giggled.

Humming, I swayed my hips against him. "Would you like to know what I'm thinking about right now?"

"Knowing you, something dirty and decidedly wicked."

Fluttering fingers to the tops of my breast, I batted my lashes. "You flatter me, Master."

He chuckled.

"But the truth is..."

Deliberately letting those thoughts dangle, I bent down so that now my face was mere inches from the line of his zipper.

He sucked in a deep breath. "Holy Calypso," he grunted.

Patting his thigh, I smiled. "I'm here, Dead Boy. I'm here." Then, unzipping him, I pulled his engorged flesh from its hiding place and kissed the very tip of it.

I purred at its velvety softness. I'd had a feeling I'd enjoy my first taste of male flesh.

His eyes rolled back, which I took to mean, "take me, baby, I'm ready."

I took him, humming like I'd once seen a whore do, kissing and licking and feasting and treating it very much like I would a lolli. His taste was divine: raw masculinity with just a dash of death. Perfecto.

He came not too soon after, shouting his release, but I was far from done with him. Moving back up, I popped a hard kiss to his lips so that he could taste his essence on me.

His groan was hungry, his movements nearly delirious.

"Shove that stake into me," I whispered against him.

"Thalassa." His voice sounded strained. "I am only a man, and you've worn me—"

"You're a god." I touched his cock, shoving power through my touch and making him stand ramrod again. "Now saddle up and ride me, stallion."

"You make no sense, but gods yes."

Clamping his hands onto my waist, he maneuvered his hips just slightly so that his hard length slipped into my maiden opening hidden beneath a fin.

I gasped at the rigid length of him sliding in and out.

"Oh Seren," I whispered, "this feels different."

Maidens were apparently built slightly different than humans on the inside. Who knew. There were far more nerve endings in my hooha, so each touch felt like lightning.

It was my turn for my eyes to roll.

I wilted against him, doing little more than meeting him thrust for thrust.

"Thalassa, oh goddess," he murmured, nipping at the shell of my ear with his flat but sharp teeth.

He stumbled back, carting me with him, our almost-fall broken by a vertical piece of rock poking out of the ground for him to rest his weight upon.

A terrible keening noise rang through the solitude of the gardens. The noise was mine.

I might have been embarrassed, but I felt too wonderful to care.

Hades rode me like a bucking stallion, making my breasts jiggle wildly from the bumpy ride.

I felt myself about to fragment, and this time, rather than grow scared, I relaxed into the dark pull, floating toward it happily, already knowing I'd shatter—but also knowing he'd catch me.

With a roar, he screamed my name, and I erupted. And just as I knew he would, he caught me.

Hades always caught me.

Themis

I found her. As the Goddess of Justice, none could deny my entry when I was solving a case. I stared at Spring, who hung suspended in air, her eyes closed, deep in slumber.

Though I was blind, I could see, not with my eyes, but through a sort of second sight. She was as lovely as she always was. A cool breath of new life.

She was well. Not a scratch on her.

But my heart sank.

Hades was guilty of this crime. Not of murder. But he'd brought Spring here. Judgment would need to be handed out.

Aria, keeper of Spring's body, looked at me.

"You know why he did this, don't you?"

Never taking my eyes off Spring, I nodded slowly. "I know."

"You can sentence him, Themis, as is your right to do. But were I you," the element of Air personified turned to me, "I'd think on this long and hard. Sometimes the punishment does not fit the crime."

Deep in my heart, I knew that this time, she was right. Zeus would not like this. Closing my eyes, I hung my head. "I will think on what you've said. Thank you, Aria."

Hades

I closed my eyes after staring at the same pattern on the coral ceiling of my temporary bedroom in Calypso's temple.

We'd returned several hours ago from our excursion into her gardens, and as always, she'd disappeared soon after.

I'd searched for any sign of her outside my window, but after an hour, I gave it up as a lost cause. Whatever she was about, she wasn't here. I felt the absence of her in the waters keenly.

Sensing a sudden oppressive surge of power, I opened my eyes just in time to see Aphrodite's watery form materialize. She floated above me, her hair undulating on the gentle current.

"Hello, Under Lord," she chirped, "how's it hanging? And by that I mean, has she totally satisfied you, or do I need to take care of business?"

I glanced at my soft phallus. "What do you think?"

Dite could force me to "get it up," as Calypso would say (it was within her power to do so, after all), but without the inducement of magic behind it, it seemed my cock cared to rise for only one female.

"Yes, well, I would be insulted, but she is quite the horny little she-devil. Who knew she had it in her?" She giggled, seeming both amused and mildly surprised. "Anyway," she flicked a wrist, "I came to update you. Themis has hidden herself away in her cave. None of us are exactly sure what Crazy's got going on, but she doesn't want anyone around right now."

Those words had me cocking my head. Themis only hid in her cave when she was trying to make sense of a dilemma. My case was cut and dried, or so I'd thought.

"Mind telling me why?" She gave me huge owl eyes. Aphrodite was no one's fool; I could sense she suspected much more than what she let on. But she also refused to speak first.

I shrugged. "No idea."

"Hm. Well, if you don't want to answer that question, how about telling me why Calypso is currently raging on Olympus."

I sat up. "She's what?"

Aphrodite laughed. "What? She didn't tell you where she planned to go today?"

"Not a word." I thinned my lips, wondering what she was about and why.

"How odd. Apollo's furious, threatening to scorch the Earth if she doesn't leave now. But that woman is wild and crazy and just a little bit amazing. Honestly. I would *hate* to be on her bad side. Anyway, tootles, got people to see and places to be."

"No, wait!" I reached out to grasp her elbow, but it was already too late. With a pop of displaced power, Aphrodite vanished.

The wench had told me just enough to make me crazed with questions, and now there was no one around to answer them.

"Damn you, Aphrodite!" I snapped, and the waters burbled with laughter.

Chapter 12

Calypso

Coming to Olympus was a little like swimming through a vat of maggots: unpleasant at best.

With a snap of my fingers, I created a ravishing gown of shimmering, crystal-clear water that danced with seahorses and colorful guppies, because their little tails were so feathery and beautiful and honestly, the way they zipped across my body made me look damn good.

My presence was immediately felt. The mountaintop rumbled. Hermes—wearing winged shoes, jeans, and a black muscle shirt—fluttered by.

"Zeus's little crony." I glowered at the five-foot-nothing boy of a man, who couldn't even grow facial hair. I mean, come on, I was supposed to be intimidated by that?

"Thalassa," he bowed, giving me suspicious eyes. "To what do we owe this honor?"

His eyes were probably the prettiest thing about him. Golden bronze like heated metal, they were positively enchanting. But the face that came along with it was utterly forgettable. He was also quite sweaty, and his hair looked unwashed, as though it'd been a couple days. He was usually a little cleaner than this, which made me wonder where he'd been.

No doubt gathering intel about my sex slave.

I gazed up the dizzying set of steps that led to Zeus's little slice of the sky. Olympus was as beautiful as every ancient painting had depicted it to be—actually, probably even more so.

The sky was a deep azure and the clouds white and fluffy. Trees bearing fruit of every sort grew from the fertile grounds beneath my feet. Fountains with masterfully crafted images of each god and goddess burbled while birds wheeled through the conifer-scented skies. What a pretentious, pompous, a-hole bunch of poo-poo heads.

Planting fists on my hips, I sighed. “Must I have a reason to come visit you, my little daffodil?”

He seemed completely offended, and I couldn’t help but laugh. “You’ve never come before.”

Getting bored with his suspicious ways now, I stared at my perfect nails. “I’ve only come to speak with Themis. I’m not here to start a war, *Pepe le Pew*.”

He sniffed at himself. Oh, he tried to be subtle about it, pretending to lift his arm and scratch at the side of his face with it, but I caught the not-so-subtle sniff test. He did smell.

“And where have you been lately, if you don’t mind *my* asking?” I smiled sweetly, giving him a face that clearly said, “See, you can trust me.”

But apparently my sweet face hadn’t been as sweet as I’d thought.

When he reached for his back pocket, I knew immediately he was going for his horn. With one mighty blow, he’d call all the ancients to attention. I’d have an angry mob on my hands if I let him blow it.

Flicking a finger, I gathered particles of water from the air itself until they formed into a spear and aimed it squarely at his heart.

“Blow that thing and I’ll stick you like a pig.”

His hand quivered.

“Now, leave me pass, or I’ll—”

“Calypso!” Apollo’s voice thundered through the very heavens, and I groaned.

I’d almost forgotten about the tiny palace-flooding incident. Chariot Boy had not, however.

His golden chariot raced across the sky, dragged by two flaming horses I liked to call Gassy and Gassier, as they were known to pass gas with some regularity. Something to do with the particular brand of fire oats Apollo fed them.

They were within five yards of me when Apollo dropped from his chariot with all the grace of an eagle in flight. He was truly a magnificent man—ideally masculine and yet with a touch of femininity to his face that softened his otherwise harsh features, making him delectable eye candy.

He lifted a fist. "You drowned my fire orchard, you venomous bitch!"

His face twisted into a snarl, and I yawned. "Apollo, are you not my friend? For I don't think I could bear it if you weren't."

Flame haloed his golden head, heating the very air and making my own water sizzle.

The little seahorses and guppies scattered to the back of me.

I grinned. "Oh, is it playtime, pet?"

Lifting my hands, I sucked the moisture from his lungs, and his lips parted as he clutched at his chest. Immediately the temperature lowered as Fire Head's wrath cooled.

"Would you like to breathe again, Apollo?"

His nostrils flared with fury, but he nodded.

"Then apologize to my babies." I glanced down at my gown, where my guppies were now quivering with fear.

When I shoved the water back into his body, he took a deep breath, glared murderously back at me, and refused to say anything.

I swear, I was going to pull that idiot over my knees and give him a good spanking, when suddenly a thick black fog rolled between us, immediately obscuring Apollo from sight.

But I sensed rather than saw that the fog had actually enveloped me. Not to hurt me though; it was almost a shield.

How odd.

"Hurt her or hers, Apollo, and so help me, you'll live to regret it." Hades' words were a ghostly echo around me.

I smiled. The darkness was him. What a lovely fool to come to my rescue as he had, though I'd certainly not needed rescuing. I wasn't quite sure how he'd shown up here, but I knew my sex slave when I heard him.

"Unbind me, Hades," I commanded.

Immediately the darkness eased up, and I was able to peek out from between thick bands of shadow to witness that not only were Apollo and Hermes here but now too were Aphrodite and Zeus.

I waved at Dite, who waved cheerily back at me. She was dressed in a red leather halter-top-style gown with a vertical slit that ran from her ankle all the way up to her breast line and was held in place by a scrap of fabric at her hipbone.

Hm. I wondered if I could get her to let me borrow that someday.

"What in the hell are you doing here, Hades?" Zeus snapped, his big, beefy body completely nude and on display.

The tip of his comically long penis glistened. Which meant either (A) he'd been getting pleasured by one of his many slaves, as everyone knew he and Hera never screwed anymore, or (B) he'd been pleasuring himself.

I voted for (B). I mean, who wanted to sleep with that goat-faced brute willingly? Well, unless you were a nymph and didn't much care what stuck its tab into your slot so long as you got tabbed good.

Nymphs were so shallow.

"I've broken no rule." My lover's deep voice put Zeus's high-pitched quack to shame.

Okay, so maybe I was being unfair. It wasn't really high-pitched or ducky sounding, but he was just so disgusting to me that it was hard to think kindly of the louse.

"You were to remain in the waters."

"And there I am." Hades' voice shook with power.

I wagged a hand through the shadow. "He's right." I said. "Not physically present means still following the rules."

I felt rather than saw Hades chuckle.

"You speak when you are spoken to!" Zeus thundered back at me.

I gasped, jaw hanging open. He did *not* just talk to me like that. I was ready to charge him, but a wall of shadow suddenly hardened in front of me so that I could not move through it.

"Allow me," Hades intoned, and then, as if a quiver of arrows had just been released, bolts of shadow drilled through Zeus's middle.

And then there was chaos. Utter, violent, land-roaring, sky-splintering-with-lightning, shrieks-of-grizzly-violence, fire-spewing-from-the-very-depths-of-the-universe chaos.

Two of the most powerful gods going *mano a mano* with each other, and all over little ol' me. It was just about enough to make a girl want to titter with delirious excitement. Of course, I wasn't really a girl, and I didn't titter. Ever.

But I did let the two beasts play because it was fun to watch.

I was safely cradled from the storm in Hades' shadow blanket, so I took a seat, called a little bowl of popcorn to me, and watched with a goofy smile on my face.

Aphrodite came and found me a moment later. "Give me some of that," she said then reached into my bowl and tossed some in her mouth. "Mm. It's good."

"I know," I said. "I'm a great cook now."

We watched in silence for a moment, and then her grin grew wide.

I have never seen Hades act like this over anyone.

Zeus's mountaintop crumbled, sending thick piles of rock to the ground, knocking down a couple of trees. The ghostly wails of the dead came shooting out of the ground like a mama giving birth to a babe. Up they came, heeding their master's command.

I was so turned on right now. He was so hawt.

So why did he trick Persephone if he didn't want her? I asked.

I hadn't realized the question had been bothering me until I'd asked it. Hades was an amazing catch. Why had he resorted to such trickery?

She frowned. *Hun, don't you know the truth? I mean, the story is really old now, but still, someone should have set you straight on this eons ago.*

"You got this, sex slave," I rooted my boy toy on when Zeus slapped at his shadow with ten thousand volts of lightning, sparking up the sky with a violence that looked as though a nuclear bomb had just been dropped on the place.

Hades shook the marbles loose from his head, gave me an answering grin, and then they were right back at it.

What story? I shoved a handful of popcorn in.

Persephone fabricated the entire tale. Hades fed her, yes. As he would have to feed any of us who showed up at his door unexpectedly, because that's who he is. Persephone ate of the fruit, then ran home that night and told her mother that Hades had not only deflowered her but tricked her as well and that she must now spend six months out of the year with him, or her mother's cherished crops would cease to grow, as Hades would curse them all.

This was not at all the story I'd heard. *So why didn't he just call the chit out as a liar?*

At this Dite's eyes looked sad. *Because by then he'd fallen in love with her. That part of the tale was true. Hades fell madly for Spring. She was his opposite in every way, and I think that youthful innocence was the attraction. In many ways, you are just like Persephone. Or rather, what he'd believed her to be at the time. Desirous that others should not see her in an ugly light, he played along with her ploy.*

The fury of the fight was dying down. This hadn't been a true war, not in the sense that they actually meant to exterminate life. More just boys blowing off steam.

Then he's an idiot.

And I said that kindly, because even though what he'd done had been foolish in the extreme, it only proved what I'd suspected of the brute all along. He was an honest-to-god gentleman. Would wonders never cease?

Go easy on him, Calypso. He was young then, relatively speaking. He thought with time she'd grow out of her wild ways. She never did.

Turning to Aphrodite, I looked her in the eye. And I saw truth shining back at me. *How is it, then, that you know this and no one else does?*

Her smile was soft. *I am the Goddess of Love. I know all things concerning matters of the heart.*

Then why didn't you tell others the truth? I wasn't angry with her, but it seemed unfair the reputation Hades had developed, especially in light of the fact that it'd been entirely undeserving.

He is a proud man and would not have wanted me to.

You know what's happened to Persephone, don't you?

There I do not. He fell out of love with Spring millennia ago. I've not been able to read Hades for quite some time.

And now?

She said nothing for a while. But she grabbed my hand and squeezed. *And now I can. Tell me, Sea, why are you in Olympus?*

To discover some truths.

I'd learned far more today than I'd expected, but I wasn't done yet. Standing, I nodded at both Hades and Zeus, who were now panting and thoroughly spent; it seemed even shadow could tire out.

"Go home and await me, Master," I said to Hades. "I am perfectly fine now."

His smile was broad. Even in shadow form, he still managed to steal my breath.

"You truly are the worst slave in the history of ever." His deep, wicked voice had my thighs tingling.

Blowing him an air kiss, I banished him. Then, turning to Zeus, I lifted a brow. "You look like you tried to rut a bull and the bull won."

"Calypso, I should roast you and make furniture of your bones."

"Whatever, dipstick. I'm off to speak with her royal blindness, and then I promise I'll be out of your hair."

With a curtsy that was far more impudent than humble, I took my leave of them.

Oddly enough, no one bothered me after that affair. It could be a handy thing to have Death be my pet, it seemed.

I came to Themis's cave home not even an hour later. Loud music emanated from the very walls of the cave itself. For a cave, the place was far from dank and honestly quite cozy. The rock was a splendid color of dusky rose, gems of all sorts veined all through it. It was dark—no doubt because Themis had no need of light—but walking down the entrance, I soon found myself in a large cave with throw rugs on the floor, comfy couches shoved up against the wall, and natural trees that'd grown up from the dirt.

Themis was dressed in blue jean shorts and a colorful crop top and was currently dancing her booty off, shaking her groove thang from one spot to the next.

Immediately she stopped and clapped her hands, and the music died. Then she took a quick sniff.

"Calypso? What are you doing here?" she asked still without turning.

Themis suddenly twirled on me and I finally got my first good look at the blind goddess. Whenever I'd seen her before, she'd always looked standoffish and aloof, dressed in a white toga with her perpetual white ribbon around her eyes.

But today her long brown hair spilled in soft waves down her back, and the opalescent whites of her eyes practically gleamed in a not-so-unattractive face.

Shoulders straightening, she shook her head. "I know why you're here."

I shrugged, tossing up my hands. I hadn't actually woken up this morning with the intention of coming up here, but after my afternoon delights, the idea had hit me like a flash.

"I have discovered where Persephone is."

I frowned. Then why hadn't she announced her verdict already?

She sighed. "Because the matter is rather more complicated than I'd anticipated."

Complicated? My mind was buzzy with possibilities.

"You really should ask him. I'm sure he'll tell you if he wants you to know."

Now it was my turn to sigh. So much for my intentions of not allowing matters to become complicated. But after his confession last night and now this, did I really have any other options?

"I'm not quite sure how to pass judgment on this one, to be honest. So I'm dancing. I find music to be very soothing when my mind is ill at ease."

This sounded more serious than I'd imagined.

"This is very serious and must be handled delicately. Truth is, I plan to leave Hades with you through the entirety of the allotted time. Calypso, I may have need of your services in the future. Would you mind?"

Did that mean there was a possibility of saving Hades?

"Quite possibly."

Then I was certainly willing to help.

Themis's smile grew wide. "You are welcome to visit me whenever you'd like. Most excellent talk, goddess fair."

"Yes, I thought so too." With a finger wave, I took my leave of her.

Chapter 13

Hades

We collapsed on a heap upon the bed, our bodies soaked with sweat and my heart still galloping like the hooves of my Night steads. I expected Calypso to vanish as she often did after sex, but she seemed in no rush to leave this night.

It'd been a week since her visit to Olympus. I'd hoped that at some point she would speak to me about what she'd done there and, more specifically, why she'd gone to Themis, but she never had.

She'd simply taken my body and had her way with me, over and over and over again.

But I had no cause to complain.

Rolling onto my side, I draped a leg over hers. "Now you're trapped and cannot leave me."

Luminescent eyes sparkled up at me. Today her form was that of water. I found I enjoyed any form she came in. Trailing a finger down the column of her throat, I smiled as diamond-encrusted clear lashes feathered like a delicate fan upon her cheeks.

"Hades," she mewled, and my gut clenched.

I was growing positively addicted to this temptress. "Thalassa."

She pretended to gag, but only briefly, and only in jest. She no longer sassed me for calling her such. In fact, she seemed to brighten whenever I did. In the privacy of our quarters, I found that name was mine alone. Just like this woman was. Only mine, ever.

Unable to resist the touch of her, even though she'd just ridden me a minimum of eight times straight, her perky breasts bouncing prettily for each ride, I cupped one of the overflowing mounds and squeezed.

She groaned. "By Olympus, I love your touch."

I froze. It was the first time she'd used that word in any context with me. But my little spitfire rarely used words properly, so I was likely overthinking things.

"But, Death Boy," she grabbed my hand, forcing me to pause in my exploration of her cool nipple, "we should talk."

Groaning, I released her and tossed myself back on the pillow, folding my arms behind my head. "Your timing, as ever, is impeccable, slave."

Giggling softly, she wiggled her pliant body atop mine. She weighed practically nothing, but I felt each and every lush curve of her.

"Ply you with sex and then talk your ear off. Yes, I know, my dear, I'm an adept student."

"Student?" I lifted a brow. "I don't think you were ever a student."

Moving an arm, I dropped it onto the curve of her buttocks where hip met thigh and squeezed. I should have been sated, but if she gave me even the slightest indication of willingness, I'd not say no.

However, it seemed she really did wish to talk. With a sigh, I moved my hand up, tracing with my finger the dimples that kissed her back.

Nibbling her bottom lip, she seemed unsure about where to start, but her fingers continued to idly stroke my longest and deepest scar, a horizontal one that ran from one side of my navel to the other.

I'd known for some time that she was curious about them.

"The scars?" I guessed.

She took in a deep breath. "I mean, if you don't want to talk about them..."

What that pause actually meant was "talk about them."

Kissing the crown of her forehead, I crossed my ankles, enjoying the feel of her naked body pressed to mine. This almost felt more intimate than the marathon sex sessions we'd been having for the past week in a half.

"When a mortal dies, they come to me, and their soul is weighed. Heavy souls go to Tartarus, light souls to the Elysian Fields."

Crossing her hands underneath her chin, she nodded. "Proceed."

My lips twitched. "If your soul is wicked, you remain as you were in death. Your injuries remain your own. But in Elysia, you are healed. Given a clean slate."

Her touch was delicate as she nuzzled at a scar just beneath my right nipple. It was small and slightly puckered.

"But that does not come without cost to you, does it, sex slave?"

Rubbing an idle hand up and down her spine, I shook my head. "No, it does not. In order for one to be cleansed, another must be defiled."

"So you don't have to take on their injuries?"

I stopped moving my hand, lost to her hypnotic eyes. "No. But I would not wish this fate upon others. It is not fair."

"And yet you would choose to allow your own beautiful body to grow deformed by it. What did this?"

She once more nuzzled the pucker.

"A girl, quite young. Early teens maybe. She'd been shot by a brother."

Calypso frowned, and I could read the fury igniting through her blood. I smoothed a finger across her furrowed brow.

"It is not what you imagine, Thalassa. The boy was a child, and the wound was little more than accident. A terrible, costly one, but an accident nonetheless."

Frowning prettily, she pressed a tender kiss to the spot. "Why are you so good?"

I snorted. "I am not always good. Many of the stories you've heard of me are true. I have a terrible temper."

She shrugged. "Nothing wrong with a bad temper."

"And a surly disposition in the morning if I've not been fed immediately."

"Magic fingers," she snapped.

I laughed. "You are determined to dress me as something I am not."

Her smile turned soft. "But maybe...maybe to me you are."

With those words, my little dove vanished.

But I smiled, because I knew that today, we'd just had another breakthrough. And since tomorrow was my day, I already knew the plans I had in store for my flighty, sharp-tongued shrew.

Calypso

I couldn't seem to stop smiling the next morning. It'd felt very wicked to rest in Hades' arms last night. I'd wanted to stay there forever. It was becoming harder and harder to remember why that was a bad thing.

All this nonsense of not wanting to get attached. Surely there was nothing wrong with a little attachment—if handled properly, that was.

But then I remembered the whole problem with Persephone, and my smile turned upside down. Themis hadn't gotten in touch with me since that day, and even Dite had stopped visiting.

The old adage that no news was good news was bulldung.

By the time I got to Nim's kitchen, I was positively cross. Jeffery came in at a certain point, took one look at me, tucked legs, and ran.

That almost made me laugh.

By the time Nimue came to find me for lunch, I was surly, no bones about it.

"This salad is wonderful, Janita. Sea kelp and sesame seeds. You're such a clever cook."

Even her words failed to bring a smile to my lips, a sight she immediately noted.

"Okay, spit it."

I opened my mouth wide. "I've got nothing in there."

"That's not what I mean." She drummed her coral-pink-lacquered nails on the tabletop. "I mean you're acting strange, and I know something's wrong, so tell me."

I shrugged. "It's Harold."

She squinted. "Who? Do you have another lover?"

"What?" I asked in a daze. "Of course I don't have another lover. What would give you such an odd idea?"

"Gee, I don't know." She lifted her brows, gave me a crooked smile, and then patted my hand. "What's wrong with... Harold, was it?"

"Of course it's Harold. Nimue, are you ill?"

She patted her belly. "Pregnancy fog. Don't mind me."

"Anyway," I batted my wrist, "I want him."

"Last I heard, you had him."

"I know. I can hardly understand meself right now. 'Tis maddening." I looked to her. Nim was always so wise, giving me great advice. Advice I hadn't heeded much lately, to be sure, but solid advice nonetheless.

She turned her palm over, asking me to proceed.

"He's leaving soon. I thought I would be okay with this."

"I take it you are not."

I crossed my arms. "No. I isn't."

Bloody poop, I wished I hadn't adopted this goddessawful accent for Janita. I was having a helluva time remembering how she spoke today. I was a mess. My head was a swirl of questions.

I wanted to storm Olympus and demand Themis give me answers now.

The water at my tail frothed. Realizing I was about to lose control, I took several swallowing breaths. I would not level my daughter-in-law's home.

"Last we spoke about this, Harold had done something to land himself into trouble. Has it not worked itself out yet?"

"Obviously not, or I'd not be grumping." Remembering my manners, I hurriedly cleared my throat. "Pardoning my manners, miss."

"Always forgiven, Janita." She smiled.

She looked like one of my beloved sea roses today, dressed all in shades of pink, red, white, and green as she was. With her dark curls piled high upon her head, she appeared so young and yet so wise.

When it came to matters of sea and home, I felt wise. But with this, this all-consuming obsession with Hades, I felt wildly out of my depths and unsure. I wanted to keep him with me forever and toss him far from my shores for turning my life upside down as he had.

And then I'd want to kiss him better if he landed too hard.

I was a wreck.

Sighing, I planted my chin on my hand. "There was a...erm, lawyer as such, who were supposed to get back to me about Harold's crime. But she's not gotten in touch wi' me yet, and I canna seem to stop the shakes from worrying."

"You're in love. It's sweet."

"Love." I scoffed. "This is lust, lass, plain and simple it is."

"I often find them to be one and the same." She shrugged a dainty shoulder. "First comes lust, then comes love, and before you know it, there's a wee babe in the belly and you've suddenly become a beached whale with sausage toes and terrible cravings for the oddest food combinations."

I laughed. Considering I'd had all the children I cared to have, I needn't worry about that particular problem.

"I don't know, Consort, mayhap it is the beginnings of love. I crave him. And not just his cock."

"Well, that's a start."

"His arms feel so nice. I laid in them last night, rested my head upon his chest, and listened to him talk of his past. He's remarkable, really."

"Mm. Yes, that's always my favorite part, too." A dreamy look flitted across her face. "Especially when they whisper their undying love to you when they think you're asleep. That tickles me every time."

Oh. Interesting. I stored that idea away in the vault.

"But what if he doesn't feel that way back? I mean, I've kept our relationship purely carnal."

She giggled, covering her mouth with a napkin. "I'm sure it seems that way to you, Janita, but you remember once that I told you how a first time marks your soul?"

I nodded.

"I can almost guarantee that you've been more unguarded than you imagined. If he feels the same way for you, believe me, you'll know it soon enough. It is an emotion far too powerful to hide for long."

I felt better, but only marginally. I still wondered what Themis was thinking. It was weird that I suddenly felt this stake in what happened to Hades. But now that I'd found my sex slave, I had no wish to release him for the next thousand years to the tender mercies of the vultures.

It seemed most unfair.

"Janita," Nim tapped my fingers, "If you want to know what that lawyer thinks, go ask her."

I felt the loss of time with Hades keenly. I had no wish to leave him for that long. In fact, I almost hadn't come this morning. Were it not for the burgeoning beans in Nimue's belly, I'd not have come at all, but I came daily to check in on my little buns and make sure they were as well as their mama.

"I should go to him," I finally said. "Tell Cook to clean these dishes today, Consort, I've got a man to go see."

Her laughter followed me down the hall.

Chapter 14

Hades

I felt the water stir at my back. I'd sat in bed for most of the day, reading. Calypso had an amazing library stacked high with books. I'd forgotten the simple pleasures in life, having to be daily in charge of running the Underworld.

I'd hoped at some point Persephone could have helped lighten the burden a little, but she'd never really taken to my dead as I'd hoped.

Small, delicate hands settled on my shoulders. Calypso began a slow massage, crushing her breasts to my back as she leaned over and whispered, "Guess who."

Smiling, I slipped my fingers through hers and squeezed. "Ah, Linx, good to see you again," I teased.

And received a sudden smack upside the head for it.

"Linx. Linx indeed, you fat arse."

But then she kissed the side of my jaw, and I must admit that I melted into her touch. I was growing rather addicted to my time with her. Twisting around, I rested a knee upon the edge of the mattress, and the region of my heart trembled.

Calypso looked like the goddess she was today. She wore a gown of tight-fitting water, the blue of the deepest ocean trenches. Her hair, normally a pale, wavy green, was a deep black and braided in such a way that it resembled an octopus's tentacle. A menagerie of golden aquatic animals encircled her neck, and her eyes were a startling pinprick of stardust.

Even the shape of her face was slightly altered, the eyes more sloping than typical, the lips a little softer, the jawline slightly sharper.

"You look lovely," I murmured, trailing my fingers through her thick braid, only to discover it actually was an octopus's tentacle.

Our god forms were usually unpalatable to mortals, which was why so many of us had adopted a more human appearance. But to me, she'd never looked more beautiful.

Wanting her to see me as I truly was, I let my own mask slip. She sucked in a deep breath, sculpting the planes of my face.

I knew what I looked like—the monstrous visage I hid, the angular features that'd terrified Persephone the one and only time she'd ever seen me.

But Calypso's eyes didn't fill with fright. Instead, her fingers moved upon me tenderly, as though learning me by touch.

"I've often wondered," she whispered.

"I do not frighten you?"

A curl of a smile ghosted upon her lips. "I always knew you were a Dead Boy. Now you've only confirmed my suspicions."

Chuckling, I pressed a kiss to the inside of her wrist.

"Do I disgust you, Hades?" she asked almost reluctantly, and where there'd been no fear before, I caught a glint of it now.

"You fascinate me, Thalassa, every inch of you."

Moving to her knees, she threw her arms around my waist and hugged me tight. And I couldn't move. This small woman was bringing me to my knees.

I'd barely survived the disastrous relationship that was Persephone, so the thought of building something with another woman alarmed me. But I wanted it, too. I'd always wanted it.

Kissing my lips, she breathed her life deep into my lungs. The very essence of her, it was cool and sweet, and I craved more of it. I was ready to cast off my clothes and do with her as I willed, but Calypso laid a steadying palm against my chest and sighed as she broke our kiss.

I frowned. She'd never stopped me before.

"Hades, where is Persephone?"

"I was ready to tell you before and you stopped me." She'd mentioned there being spies around, but I'd suspected strongly it'd been more than that.

The downward turn of her lips confirmed my suspicions.

"I was scared, Hades."

"Why?"

Her eyes grew wide. "Because you terrify me. Being with you. The things you make me feel. It wasn't supposed to be this way."

"What do I make you feel?"

Scooting back against the headboard, she crossed her legs at the ankles, and I couldn't help but trace my finger down the inseam of her bare left foot. She grinned, wiggling her toes.

"Small."

Not what I'd expected to hear. "Small? I take it this is no compliment."

She sighed again. Calypso was rarely this serious, and when she was, it always bothered me. Moving to the footboard, I pressed my back against it so I could look squarely at her and she at me. We gazed at one another in silence, our heads full of many thoughts.

"I'm the waters of life, Hades. I am vast. There is no place on Earth or Kingdom that I do not exist. I am a mighty force, and yet with you, I feel so..." she rolled her wrist, as though seeking the right word.

"Exposed?" I guessed, pausing in my touch of her. I felt the first bite of that emotion I'd so often felt with Persephone but that'd been entirely absent during my time with Calypso. The blow of it twisted my stomach into knots.

"What? No." She huffed, as though I were a fool.

But I'd been down this road too many times to count. Persephone had always had "talks" with me. Chats about how her needs weren't being met, when in fact, none of mine were. We'd never slept together. She was as unspoiled today as she'd ever been before my supposed rape of her.

"Then what?"

"I don't know. Gods," she rolled her eyes, "my words so often confound me. You make me feel like a woman, Hades, I suppose is what I'm trying to say."

It was my turn to frown. "Calypso, you've always been a woman."

"Yes, but not really. I am an elemental. One of the four great elementals. That is who I am. Always needed and yet often taken for granted. When you gather together on Olympus, have I ever been invited?"

"Thalassa, you've never wanted to come." I shook my head, sure that I was missing something here.

Her eyes crossed, and I had to admit, that even when irritated, she was cute. Smiling now, however, would probably be doing myself no favors.

"That's not the point though, because I've never been asked. You all sit on your high and mighty thrones while I supply you with practically everything."

"That is not so—"

She held up a finger. "When Hephy has to make Zeus his bolts, does he or does he not need to dip his metals in water?"

"Well—"

Not to be deterred, she pressed on. "And when Bacchus makes his wine, where do you think that water comes from? Not Psycho, I can promise you that. And Aphrodite's countless baths that makes her skin sparkle, Demeter's crops, your dead, all of it, *all, of, it,* done by my hand."

I was confused. I thought we'd been talking about Persephone, so I couldn't quite figure how we'd wound up here. I scratched the back of my head.

"The point is, Hades, I dismissed you all as vain, selfish, and petty, ridiculous creatures, and now you're making me think that I've been wrong. Not about all of you. Most of you really are vain, selfish worms—"

I cleared my throat.

She chuckled. "You, Dite, and Themis are the exceptions to the rule." She shrugged. "I'm learning that I don't know everything, that there are still things that surprise me, and—"

Crawling to her knees, she made her way toward me. Then, parting her thighs, she straddled my legs, looking deep into my own eyes. Not for sex. There was nothing at all sexual about this. Calypso wanted honesty from me, true baring of emotions. And I knew that if I gave it to her, my entire life would forever change.

"You most of all."

My lashes fluttered. "Thalassa, I'm—"

Grabbing my chin, she forced my eyes to hers. "If I'm going to put my neck on the line for you, Hades, then I want to know you're worth it."

What exactly did that mean? I wasn't asking her to fight my fights. I didn't need her to do it. Clenching my jaw, I twisted out of her grasp. "I'm not some child that needs coddling, woman."

She punched me. Reared back and walloped my bicep hard enough that it throbbed. Twin dots of pink stained her porcelain cheeks. "You don't get to decide that. I do. You're coming to mean too much to me."

I snorted. "My cock does, I'm sure." I thrust up, stabbing her rear with it.

"Mm." She nodded quickly. "Yes, I enjoy that part of you. Very much. But..."

Pulse suddenly pounding like a raging river in my ears, I waited with bated breath for her to continue. When she didn't, I snapped, "But?"

Palming my chest, she shook her head. "Damn you, Death Boy, but there are other parts to you I want to explore. Like your soul. Your heart. I wish to know you, bastard of a man, more than just riding your cock—which is exquisite. You have consumed me. I think of you day and night, and not just riding your bean pole. I want to know what your favorite color is. I believe it's black, but—"

"Amethyst."

Her lips turned to a tiny "o." "I'd never have guessed. Or your favorite flower."

"Nightshade."

She sighed. "That is a lovely flower. But that's the thing of it, we have four days left together, and it's not enough. Not nearly. Do you desire to know me as I desire to know you, Hades? This is what I need to know."

I should say no, spare her feelings. I'd tried and failed miserably at romance. She would someday grow to hate me as Persephone had, and with Calypso, I wasn't sure I was strong enough to bear it.

She sank claws into my chest, cutting through my flesh near to the bone, and bled me. "Do not lie to me, Death, you reek of it."

The mask of her face turned deadly.

"I said nothing, Thalassa," I said, slowly disengaging her claws from my body. Instantly the wounds healed. She'd given me naught but a love scratch.

"Answer me, or I'll take your head, you devil," she snarled, and the waters began to turn murky with threads of green.

Chuckling, I rolled my eyes. "Must you always be so dramatic, woman? You wish to know the truth? Then yes. Yes, okay, I want you. I want all of you. I want nothing more than to rip this godforsaken dress off your body and taste my fill of you. But I want more than that. I want to take you through my home, I want to show you my people, I want you to be a part of my life, in the Underworld. Do you understand the impossibility of our situation? Not to mention the fact that I will be locked up soon. You and I both know this."

Grunting, she crossed her arms. "Do you think so little of me, bastard, that you honestly believe I'd let something so minor hold me back? Have I not flooded the very heavens before? I could take Zeus's golden crown if I wanted it. I am far beyond this weak, silly woman sitting like a peahen on your cock."

I laughed. I did adore her ridiculous ways.

"But you have yet to answer my question. Where is Persephone? She is not dead; Themis told me so. So what did you do to her?"

"I poisoned her and banished her to the realm of Air."

She frowned, and the transformation that overcame her I wished I could paint. The way her brows dipped and then slowly rose, how her eyes had darkened and then began to glitter with humor, how her lips were currently wobbling as though withholding laughter, and how it all suddenly coalesced at once into a giant peal of laughter that bubbled from her lips and rocked the very waters of the seabed.

It took her a moment to gather herself, and once she did, she was wiping tears from the corners of her eyes. "I was so wrong about you. I thought you'd had no hand in this. Where did you get the snail?"

I smirked. "Charon made a deal with a maiden."

"And here I blamed Poseidon."

"Well," I shrugged, "maybe I was trying to throw Themis off the scent a little with that deception."

"And the blood? Cerberus missing?"

"The blood was Cerberus's." I blinked, remembering the grizzly set of events that'd led me to finally taking a stand against Persephone's wild ways.

She shook her head. "But there was so much blood. Dite said the dog had been found."

"She lopped off his third head. She wanted to hurt me, and she did."

"Oh, poor puppy," she mourned.

Only Calypso could call the slobbering killer a poor puppy. Cerberus was a monster through and through. With a taste for trespassers, he was my first line of defense against the constant scheming and trickery of my brothers. Neither of them cared to possess the Underworld, and yet they'd always resented my godhead and would happily see me dispossessed from my kingdom.

"It will grow back, eventually."

She was back to cuddling me now, twining her fingers languidly through the ends of my hair on the nape of my neck. The touch broke my flesh out in goose bumps.

I'd seen and possessed the woman every which way imaginable, and yet this was the type of intimacy I'd secretly always yearned for: an ear to listen and a heart that cared.

It was those feelings that caused both Zeus and Poseidon to view me as weak, as less than them. But I'd never cared for the debauched lifestyle of my brothers. I'd always been far more private than they. Nor did I care to sire a million bastards, as they'd each done. I wanted any offspring from my bloodline to know their parentage.

"Why did she do that?"

"Why does Persephone ever do what she does?" I shrugged. "I told Demeter that she needed to check her, needed to set boundaries, but she never did. Persephone was unhappy, self-centered, and spoiled. I gave her everything I had to try and keep her happy—jewels, clothes, money, even my time—but always she mocked and laughed in my face."

"Why did you accept her as your responsibility, Hades? You have allowed everyone to believe you raped her, stole her innocence from her. Why?"

I sighed. I'd often asked myself that question, and the only answer I could give was, "Because I imagined myself in love. I wanted to protect her from herself."

"You could tell Themis what she did to the dog. Surely that would justify your banishment of her."

I shrugged. "What would be the point? Everyone believes the lies now. Her reputation is untarnished. While mine..."

Kissing me, she pressed her warm body tight to mine. The kiss was short, but it held a breath of meaning.

"What deal did you make with my sister to get her to agree to take on Persephone?"

Aria hadn't been pleased when Cerberus had suddenly shown up in her realm carting the sleeping body of Spring. But just like Thalassa, Air was in all things. She'd heard Persephone's lies and knew the girl for what she was.

"I imagine she took pity on me."

She blinked. "Spring cannot stay there forever. Soon she'll be required to return to the Earth."

Running fingers through my hair as the exhaustion of the past few days suddenly seemed to catch up to me, I shook my head. "I couldn't stand her in my realm for another hour. I didn't think. I simply reacted. She'd gone too far this time."

"Oh, Hades," her shoulders slumped, "the effects of the snail are temporary. She'd come out of the coma soon enough. You need to tell someone the truth."

"I do, and she's returned to me. I cannot bear the sight of her right now."

"And yet you would allow yourself to be cast into torment. What an idiot you are, my dear."

Her words were sharp, but her kiss was sweet.

"I have an idea, Death Boy." She patted my chest. "But tonight, I am tired. So do with me as you will."

Tossing her arms over her head, she yawned loudly, and I could see that she really was tired.

"Thalassa, all I wish of you tonight is to stay with me until the light returns."

Grabbing a fistful of my shirt, she dragged me to the head of the bed, shoved the sheet down with her foot, and, with a heavy exhalation, vanished her gown.

And for just a moment, with all her curves on display to my greedy gaze, I wanted to take it all back and have my way with her. But then somehow I was beneath the blanket and without clothes on, and her sweet scent invaded my senses as she snuggled into my side.

"I thought you'd never ask, Bubble Butt," she murmured sleepily.

I smiled, kissed the crown of her head, and imagined sleep would elude me the rest of the night with the feel of her pressed so tight. But I slept like a baby, and it was glorious.

Calypso

I awoke to the feel of a slumbering dragon resting on top of me. I was about to kick the beast off when I realized it was only Hades snoring like a banshee.

"Aww, you're so adorable," I whispered, unable to help from wiggling my bottom.

A thick, sharp cock pressed into me. "Move like that again, and I'll toss you on your back."

"Oh." I wiggled harder, and he did just as he threatened to do. Before I knew it, he was wedged in tight between my thighs and staring at me in way that made me feel unbalanced, off kilter, and absolutely freaking amazing.

Flicking at his nose, I huffed. "Get off me, you beast."

"No." He settled in, rubbing himself between my thighs as he languidly kissed a hot trail down the side of my neck.

I moaned, rutting his cock even as I shook my head. "No seriously, let me up."

Realizing I wasn't just saying that, he finally stopped and pulled back, staring at me with a quizzical brow. I whimpered. He hadn't needed to stop that quickly.

Wrapping my arms around his back, I forced him back down and humped his still-bulging bit of anatomy.

"Thalassa, what are you doing?" he asked in a slow, syrupy voice that had me seeing stars.

I continued to rub harder. A little bit more to the left and I'd be there. I wiggled my bum until he was pressed more fully to the spot, and then I proceeded to "rub one out," as they say. Now that phrase I understood all too well.

Hades let me do my thing, because that's what Hades did. But he'd not moved, only continued to gaze at me with a perturbed frown. Sighing with satisfaction, I pulled him down to me for a kiss, which he quickly if not brusquely returned before growling in his chest.

"Well, what a way to start a morning," I chirped, and scooted out from under him.

"Thalassa!" he snapped when I sauntered toward the door with my rear exposed to all the world. "You're going to just leave me like this?"

Flinging the door wide, I grasped the edge of it and grinned at him. "They say waiting makes the heart grow fonder—or, in your case, the balls bluer." I shrugged. "I've got places to be and idiots to save you from. So just wait for me. But don't touch yourself!" I warned with an eyebrow raise. "I'll know if you do, and you'll pay."

He curled his lips and leaned back on his hands. "Oh yeah, how?"

The way the blanket draped over his hipbones hid nothing from my view, but it did make him look much more naughty and had me sweating above the brow.

Damn, he was hawt.

"Do you like carrots, lover?"

Frowning, he shoved fingers through his thick dark hair. Swarthy skin, rippling, bulging biceps with veins that poked out...my gods, he was delicious. And absolutely all mine. I'd decided that last night.

I'd fight to the death for him.

"Not particularly," he frowned.

"Well, I wasn't intending them to be eaten, silly boy." I winked and then, with a toodle-loo, vanished to Linx's stables.

She lifted her head from where she'd been slumbering, a basket of half-eaten sea fruit beside her.

Her smile was knowing.

"What?" I asked, trying to hide my grin, but I was losing that battle.

Are we keeping him, then?

"Well, duh."

Patting my hair into place, I twirled with my arms spread wide, asking without words how I looked. Hades liked me in my more primal form, and so I would head to Olympus today looking like the beautiful freak I was. I'd even managed to manufacture a dress for myself that I imagined Dite might wear. It had cutouts beneath the breasts, above the stomach, and at the hips. It was crafted of white glowworm silk and was a bit more diaphanous than what Lust typically seemed to want to wear, but I figured in this, I looked like the powerful goddess I was. But just to seal the deal, I crafted a tiara of pure gold with sea urchin spines jutting up from it and placed it just so on my head.

It was time to remind those a-holes just how much of a bitch I could really be when I was angered.

Lovely as ever, sister mine.

"Naturally," I inclined my head then turned to go but remembered something. "Oh, and Linx, be a dear and lock our gates. I've a feeling our waters might float with bodies for a while."

What in the world have you got planned in that lovely head of yours?

"Just a little bit of hell."

Then, with a wink and an air kiss, I vanished, making a detour back to Hades' room first.

"Oh, sex slave," I chirped when I entered, delighted to see his jaw drop at my appearance.

He'd dressed back in his typical attire of black silk and loafers, impeccably groomed as ever, and I wanted nothing more than to tear his buttons off and muss him all up.

I loved that only I got to see him that way.

"Calypso?" He scrubbed a hand down his jaw.

"Close your gates to the Underworld if you would."

He could do it with his mind. Obviously he'd been too busy that one day being rustled up like a cow to the slaughter to think about it, for which I'd be eternally grateful, as I'd have never gone to visit him otherwise. What a horrible waste of a sex slave that would have been.

"Why?" His deep, deep voice shivered.

I smiled sweetly. "Because we're about to piss off some serious bumholes today."

Nostrils flaring, a grin cut one corner of his face. "Don't ever change, Thalassa."

"Why would I? I'm already perfect."

I was just about ready to leave when he said," If you ever take another lover, I'll kill him. Fair warning to you now."

"Oh, I love it when you get all caveman on me. Okay then, no other lovers. But I do have an issue with a certain Persephone thinking she's got rights to you."

"She doesn't."

"Hm." I thinned my lips, adjusting the tiara. "We'll just see about that. A girl can never be too careful with her goodies. And your goodies are my goodies, Death Boy."

He chuckled. "One last thing though before you leave. What exactly are you planning to do with carrots?"

"You really want to know?"

"I wouldn't have asked if I didn't."

"I saw a whore shove one up her john's ass. He loved it. Came in like ten seconds."

He blinked, almost looking shocked. “Hm. Well,” he cleared his throat, “if I were Apollo, I’m sure I would love it.”

“I knew it,” I snapped my fingers.

“But if you don’t mind, I think I’ll pass on the carrot, my dear.”

I shrugged. “If you say so. But it would have been fun.” I wiggled my brows.

Instantly his eyes hooded, and I could read his thoughts as if I’d heard him speak them. He was now curious. I was an excellent lover. “Ten seconds, huh?” he asked a moment later, but I only laughed and vamoosed.

Chapter 15

Calypso

Moments later, I was headed to a place no one had expected me to go, lest of all myself.

I'd not visited with my sisters in, oh, hm...years, really. Like a couple hundred thousand, give or take. We weren't really that tight. Like we were close, I guess, but we weren't *tiiiiiight,* there were no Christmas cards exchanged or birthday presents doled out. But we really couldn't live without each other either. It was a family thing. What can I say?

Wrinkling my nose, I headed to Fiera's hearth first, mainly because as my polar opposite, she was unpleasant for me to be around for too long.

Screwing my eyes shut, I willed myself to the realm of Fire. I knew the moment I'd arrived, because I began to sizzle. I had a limitless amount of water at my disposal to keep me from harm as I walked down the brimstone pathway flickering with hottest flame. Shielding myself tight, I admired my sister's decorative skills.

For as far as the eye could see, this land and everything that lived in it burned, a perpetual flame that would never be extinguished. The mountains burned. Fire oaks with their beautiful fiery leaves snapped and crackled. Fireflies with burst of flame emitting from their tiny rears flitted happily here and there.

Tiny fire imps, nasty little devils with teeth as sharp as Bruce's, bounded between trees, staring at me with wide-eyed wonder. They were dressed as wee woodcutters, with breeches that came to their knobby knees and shirts stained a permanent black.

Their hair was not actually hair at all but blue flame that writhed and danced like charmed cobras around their withered frames.

I waved merrily to a boy, no older than eight, nine thousand years at the most, who came closest to me.

"Where is Fiera?" I called out.

He licked his lips. "Ye look tasty, ye do."

Grinning, I knelt and held out my hand. "Would you like a wee nibble, little devil?"

As he hopped toward me, I could feel the eyes of those hiding still gazing on me with wonder, fear, and even a dollop of hungry jealousy.

The imp moved strangely, dragging his knuckles across the ground with each hop, reminding me oddly of a guttering candle flame. When he neared, I saw that his face had the youthful appearance of a cherubim, but his brows were nothing but soot and ash. His lips were wormy little lines and his eyes an unusual color of purple.

How adorable he was.

Cooing to him, I gave him one of my fingers. "You may nibble, but do not bite, or I shall cut your head off your neck."

"Yessum." He bobbed his head enthusiastically and then, opening his razor-sharp mouth, suckled gently on the tip of my pinky.

The touch of his tongue was fire through my bones, and I had to admit to liking the burn. Water was a delicacy in these parts and much savored. He drank his fill of me, so that his belly was nicely distended by the time he'd finished.

Then, chortling happily, he grasped my hand and beamed. I'd made a friend.

"I'll take ye to me queen," he chirped. I was about to ask him to unhand me, because the steam curling between our palms was making me feel wilty, but he was so ridiculously adorable that I that decided just this once I'd deal.

Pea Brain, as I'd soon learned he was called, blathered on and on relentlessly about how pretty I was and how fine I'd tasted, and would I come back tomorrow and feed him again?

To which I smiled but shook my head no. "If I feed you again, I would have to feed the rest of you miscreants, and I'd be here an eternity, Pea Brain. I am here but for a moment, and then I should have to leave."

I soon spied a thatched hut off in the distance. The entire thing was burning, of course.

There was a beautiful little garden out in front that looked like vegetables and fruits. I recognized a few of them: fire snap peas and charred tomatoes on the vine.

My stomach grumbled; I'd forgotten to eat this morning. I wondered if I could beg some food of my sister.

And then I spied said sister. She was as lovely as ever. Her figure was trim and toned, and she wore a buttery gown that fell past her ankles and that sparked with the light of a thousand flames.

Like the imp's, her hair was also made of fire, but this fire was green, a mystical flame that curled down her back becomingly. Her skin gleamed like burnished opal.

"Thalassa?" Fiera asked with a soft frown marring her polished skin. "To what do I owe this honor?"

Pea Brain dropped my hand then and then, dropping prostrate before his queen, chanted, "I am not worthy. I am not worthy, my flaming enchantress of beauty."

Fiera cast him a benevolent smile. "You may go now, Pea."

Scampering to his feet, he bounded off like a tiny kangaroo.

When I had her full attention again, I said, "I wish you to rain down fire on Olympus, love."

"Oh, do you?" She smiled. "And what have those fools done this time?"

The last time Fiera had done aught against them had been during the great Titan war. For reasons beyond me, she'd sympathized with the stupid brutes. They'd lost, of course, but to the best of my knowledge, she'd not bothered with the Olympians since.

"They wish to harm my sex slave."

It took her a moment to grasp what I'd said, and when she did, her opalescent eyes widened. "Thalassa, are you virgin no more?"

Giggling, I cried, "Nope!"

She clutched at her chest. "And how was it? I thought you did not desire a man's touch."

Rolling my eyes as though in ecstasy, I sighed. "Ye gods, it is glorious. His cock is a magnificent thing, and I wish to ride it for an eternity, but now the bastards threaten to torture him for a millennium at least, and I am not ready to release him. He is mine."

Perplexed wonder crossed her face. I knew my confession amazed and confused her. If I'd been her, I was sure I'd feel much the same way. There'd never been a man worthy of us.

Until now. Hades was quite worthy of me.

"I will do as you say, Thalassa. I will aid you in this, but first I desire a boon from you."

I'd come prepared, knowing I'd be asked. Nothing was ever granted without a cost.

"Yes? What do you wish?"

Her eyes narrowed into shrewd slits. "I too wish to know the wonders of a man. Help me to find one, and I am at your disposal."

I thinned my lips. "You do understand, my darling, that not all men are created equal? What you ask is a tall order. And because I have nothing but the utmost respect for you, I would see you have nothing but the best. And sadly, I have taken the best."

Mine. Mine. Mine.

She shrugged. "Second best is fine by me. I find I am curious about your male and wish to know one of my own. At least to taste one."

"Hm." I eyed her. Lovely as she was, she had one fatal flaw. "It could take some time, love. There are few in this world that could handle your heat."

She crossed her arms and tapped her foot. "A man for a boon. That is my wish."

"Done." I snapped my fingers. Surely there was someone out there who wouldn't die under her touch. And if a few lost their lives in the search, well, they clearly weren't worthy, right?

I smiled. "Now, about those tomatoes." I pointed and fanned my lashes. "Pretty please."

Thirty minutes later I shoveled the last tomato into my mouth, swallowed, and zipped myself on over to Tiera's place. For being Earth, it would have been natural to expect to see lush grass and plant life everywhere, but there was nothing but rocks.

The place was flat, barren, and utterly bland.

There were no cute little imps to nibble on my fingers. There were no rock bunnies or Chihuahuas scampering up to come greet me.

To be honest, Tiera was as dull as the place she called home.

Wrinkling my nose, I followed the dusty trail to her house, which was nothing but a circular tower of gray stones that'd been leeched of most of its color by the sun.

"Tiera," I called when I neared her steps. An "unwelcome" mat was placed on the doorstep.

It was literally unwelcoming. The words, to be more precise, said, "Leave now, or I'll eat you."

My sister was such a darling.

Tiera came out, scowling, a moment later. Her skin was pale gray, the type of color that came from rarely leaving the den she called a house. Skulking in shadow did that to a person.

She was dressed in drab colors from head to toe, and the only real color to her was her hair, a rich nutty brown she had twisted back into a tight bun that sharply revealed the harsh, straight planes of her angular face.

Tiera wasn't hideous. None of us were. But she'd never been one who cared about her appearance, either.

"What the hell do you want, Thalassa?" she snapped without preamble.

"I just wanted to say hi." I waved.

Of all my sisters, she'd be the toughest to convince. But I had a pearl up my sleeve, a little bauble she'd always wanted but I'd never quite been able to part with before.

Tiera had one weakness—precious stones. And the rarer they were, the more green with envy she became. There was one stone in particular she'd never be able to reach, as it only grew beneath my waters, and there was only one of them in existence. Oh yes, she'd play ball with me.

"No you don't, you selfish beast. You hate me and I hate you, so just tell me what you're here for and let's get this over with."

I huffed. "Well, fine, if you're going to be *that* way about it. I want you to create an earthquake through all of Olympus. Just level it to the very ground."

"No." She thinned her lips and turned to go.

"Don't you even want to know why?" I asked, racing around her so she was forced to look at me.

"Not really. Go away."

She waved her hand at me.

Gods, Tiera really needed to work on her people skills. But I was determined to save my Death Boy, and one cranky wench wouldn't stop me.

"Well, then, what if I told you I'd give you the Seren Stone for your pledge?"

She stopped, not saying anything but cocking her head.

Oh, I had the wench right where I wanted her. She smacked her lips.

The avarice was strong in her.

"Mmhmm." I shook my head, bobbing my delicate octopus braid as I did so. "All yours, and the only string is, you do my bidding when I call. I mean, really, you can't ask for a more perfect trade, now, can you?"

Her already thin lips puckered. "You've never been willing to part with that. Why now?"

"Because it's important to me?" I shrugged. She'd not wanted to know my reasons earlier, so tough kazungas, lady, I was keeping Hades my secret.

Her jaw clenched. "If you're lying to me—"

"Oh, sister." I gripped her shoulders and shook her gently. "Do you honestly think me capable—"

I stopped, remembering the Heretical Wars of 1002. Okay, so maybe she had a point.

I held up my hands. "On my honor as the Water. No tricks, no games. All I want from you is to rock their world, but only if I say so. Right now, I mostly mean to use you as a threat, but if they push me, you do it. So whaddaya say, Sis, deal or no deal?"

"What if you don't need me to level them—do I still get it?"

Dammit, she would ask that. Grumbling inwardly, I swallowed thickly and nodded reluctantly. "Of, of course, Tiera."

"You trick me, and I'll bury you."

She could try, the cold-hearted-evil-manipulative-taking-my-Seren-Stone-even-if-she-didn't-do-anything shrew! But I wasn't here to start World War III.

"You have my word." We shook on it, sealing the deal. A powerful rush of energy imploded from between our palms, rocking the land beneath our feet and shifting the stones.

Figuring now was as good a time as any to make my escape before I was accidentally on purpose flattened in a rock slide, I vamoosed on over to the final sister.

This was the one I'd held off till the end because of who she was currently hiding. I had a couple things to say to young Persephone that I didn't want my boy toy knowing.

Aria's home was as welcoming as Tiera's was not. There wasn't land, but the skies were a glorious sunny blue, and angelic sylphs winged through the skies, their songs reminding me of Gregorian chants.

The clouds were so fluffy and white, and it was instantly notable to me that Zeus depended mightily on the abilities of this sister. A gentle breeze carted the clean scent of spring on it. Flowers of first bloom, my beloved sea roses among them, saturated my lungs.

For all her flaws, Persephone could make beautiful treasures. Following the trail of her scent, I arrived in moments to my sister's castle in the sky. It wasn't built of stone or coral or any other type of common building material but rather of cumulonimbus clouds that sparkled like diamonds.

Aria, already knowing I'd arrived, daintily appeared on the drawbridge, silvery white hair and gown billowing behind her in a graceful arc.

"Sister." She smiled. "I'd halfway expected your arrival to come much sooner than now."

"Oh?" I lifted my brow.

Her smile was secretive. "I am guarding Persephone's body, after all, and the gossip in Olympus is that you've fallen rather half mad for my beloved Under Lord."

I would be jealous of her turn of phrase, but everyone knew Aria to be in love with another. She'd never admitted out and out just who that other was, but I had an idea. Though since my sister never offered up the name, I honored her wishes by keeping silent on the matter entirely.

"I suppose I have." I brushed my fingers across the sudden rainbow that arched beside me. "And now I suppose you know why I am here."

"I have my suspicions." Her grin was spun of pure delight. "But first, you may go visit with the captive, as I'm certain that is whom you greatly wish to see."

Stepping to the side, she gracefully swept a hand out so that I might walk past. Nodding my thanks, I followed the glittering staircase downward into the deepest parts of the cloud to where no light penetrated and only darkness ruled.

Down here, the gentle breezes were more like raging zephyrs slamming like fists against my body. But I was strong enough to bear it. Head held high, I continued my downward trek until I'd reached the deepest and darkest threshold and stared at the lone figure suspended before me.

Persephone had her eyes closed as though in sleep. Her rich brown skin glowed like freshly turned earth; it was that glow that allowed me to see her at all. I knew if her eyes were open, I'd see their enviable color, a very stunning shade of amethyst.

She had hair the color of ebony and a facial structure that'd once made Zeus weep to gaze upon it. There was no fault with Persephone's looks; she was spring eternal. Even down here in this pit of darkness, her flowers bloomed, covering her from head to toe in a gown of blood-red rose petals. Baby's breath threaded through her hair in winding loops.

I had never been prone to fits of jealousy; I was perfect. But I must admit to suffering a tiny pang of heart at the sight of her. Persephone was my antithesis in most every way. She'd had Hades almost since the dawn of man, and yet she'd spurned his devotion.

"Why?" I asked her, but of course, she did not answer. I continued talking. Even suspended in sleep as she was, I knew she heard me. In some recess of her mind, she was aware of my presence.

Lifting a brow, I shook my head. "He would have given you the world, and you denied him. I think I should never understand you, Sephone. I should hate you. I imagine most any goddess would. You had his complete attention and devotion nearly all your life, but no more."

I shrugged. "He truly is mine. In every way. And I do not say this to mock or tease you. It is simply fact. Should you ever wish to seek an audience with him, I would not deny you. And should you do aught to try and take him from me, well, you're welcome to try, my beauty, for I am secure in the knowledge that no other will ever turn his head again."

I'd not really known what I'd come down here to say to her, but the words pouring from my mouth made absolute sense to my heart. I could almost imagine Nimue clapping proudly behind me. I smiled.

"I will leave you with one final pearl of wisdom: the very spring and root of honesty and virtue lie in good education. That is what this is, little flower. Embrace who you were truly meant to be, stop giving into the petty and vain selfishness inherent in our kind, and grow up. Take this time to think and mature. You lost something great, and you will never get it back. Mourn the loss of him now, and when the time comes for your release, smile, for the hour of your rebirth is at hand."

With a farewell wave, I mentally patted myself on the back for a job well done.

Aria met me once I'd crested the top landing.

"You were far kinder than I'd have been." She lifted a pencil-thin brow.

"I don't know. I do not exactly care for the woman, but looking at her now, she looked so young. And it dawned on me that in many ways, she mostly is. Spring is birth. Persephone is like a young seedling, and I do hope she will grow up someday, but Hades did right by bringing her to you."

"Ah, the wisdom of the eternal waters." She brushed a thumb across my cheek. "And you should know that Hades did not bring her to me. Cerberus did, dragging her in one set of jaws. Very carefully, mind you. Even though the chit had cut off one of his heads, not a tooth punctured her body. No doubt Hades' doing."

"He is such a thoughtful brute that way." I nodded, and she laughed.

"What need you of me, sister?"

"I simply need the threat of you, my dear. And what can I give you in return?"

"An invitation to the wedding."

I hugged her. If there was a wedding, it wouldn't be for a few years yet—at least fifty or sixty years from now. I wanted to make sure that once the honeymoon phase ended, we were still a perfect match. But I answered, "Done and done."

I shook my groove thang when I entered Themis's cave of wonders. I really did like her taste in music. Today there was a cheery pop beat blasting through her home.

Dressed in Spandex workout gear, Themis twirled on the balls of her feet, a sweaty, sloppy mess but laughing effervescently. Clapping her hands, she stopped the music, and her eyes sparkled.

"Praise be. I thought you'd never come."

I raised a brow. Not like she'd called me back. I crossed my arms.

"Oh stop, pouting, Calypso. You could see my dilemma with your own two eyes. The man is as guilty as sin, and yet how could I honestly condemn him for that? I was in a pickle, and you know it."

Not the way I saw it. Anyone with two eyes could figure out that he'd done what he'd done for a reason and that goddess or no, Persephone had needed a good spanking.

"Bah." She swatted a hand. "Justice is blind and all that. Everyone tells me that I am to judge with the facts and with not my heart, but I find that organ growing softer with each passing day. I weighed Persephone's sins, and they are many. I've no wish to release her from Aria's keeping for the time being."

But if she didn't release Hades and prove he'd not killed the beast, then Zeus would still try to punish him. All knew there was no love lost between the brothers. Right or wrong, none of that mattered to Zeus. He wanted absolute authority, and Hades had always been a vexing thorn in his flesh.

She nodded. "Exactly right."

But why not just reveal that Persephone lived, at the bare minimum?

"I tell them that, and they would scour the earth and all its hidden realms to find her. They would never stop, and Hades would still be tormented. And so my quandary remains. Hades is guilty, but my scales weigh him innocent. So what do I do?"

I had spoken with my sisters, and I'd come prepared in case she planned to fight me. But I could see now that there was still a way to use our combined forces to do my will.

Themis touched the tip of her nose. "And so our thoughts finally align. You know, you really are quite fascinating to speak with. Don't be such a stranger, Calypso."

I waved. She wasn't quite so bad herself. "Yup. Till next time, bat."

My final stop brought me right to Zeus's throne room. I really hadn't been in the mood to spar with each and every a-hole. I'd hoped by seeking a private audience Zeus, I could settle terms with him, one adult to another.

He glowered at me, he was naked, and there was a woman (again, not Hera) sucking on him loudly. There was another woman behind him shoving something into something. I wasn't quite sure what, but I suspected there might be a carrot involved.

"What in the *HELL* do you want?" he thundered.

"Oh Zeus, Zeus, darling, why must we always fight so? I come not to shake the hornet's nest today. I merely come on a peacekeeping mission."

Broad nostrils flared. I could never see what women found so irresistible about him. Had to be magic. He was blinding them to his true form.

Actually, his true form was a complete mystery to most. Paintings had depicted him as a tree, once even as a swan, and as a man on many occasions, but I knew what he really looked like. I'd seen him born, after all.

But I'd vowed never to think on it again. And so I wouldn't.

The women, like the good little sycophants they were, continued to service him, their perky little breasts bobbing up and down, up and down, as they squealed and exclaimed loudly as though pleasuring him were the best thing evah.

Honestly, I adored Death Boy, but I'd had to rub one out this morning. Pleasuring another was great, but getting pleasured was even better. But, none of my business.

"Peacekeeping." He snorted as though he did not believe me. "Enlighten me, then, Calypso."

"Toss out this ridiculous charge against Hades. Let him return to his realm and do what he does best: take care of his dead."

When Zeus tossed his head back and laughed, bolts of lightning danced through his hall, filling it with the stench of ozone.

What a show-off.

"I think not." He knuckled fat tears from his eyes.

I crossed my arms, remembering that I was here for peace. Peace. *Peaccccce, ohhhhhmmmm,* I mentally chanted. "What would you do with the Underworld, then? Hades can handle it now, but add torture to the equation and you're looking at a big, fat, rotting mess. I hardly think you'd want that."

His face contorted, and I knew what was coming. I'd seen that look on Dead Boy's face a time or twenty. Curling my lip, I turned my back. I had no desire to see Zeus ejaculate rainbows, or whatever the hell he did.

Once I no longer felt the shudders roll through the floor, I peeked over my shoulder. The women were back to bobbing again, although this time they'd swapped places.

Ew.

"I've already chosen his replacement."

Oh, how very convenient. That prick didn't care if Persephone was dead or missing. His only concern was dethroning Hades. Because only Hades could actually make a power play for Zeus's throne. Well, so could Psycho, but he was Zeus's bitch in all things. But how could Zeus not realize by now that Hades had no desire to dethrone his brother?

Rubbing the bridge of my nose, I tried one last time to reason. "He's got no plans to boot you to the docks, Zeus. Your title is secure."

He lifted a brow, and at first I thought he was about to squirt out more rainbows, but I was wrong. "The gods are loyal to me. None of them would take his side, so my throne is already secure."

"Oh, you fat bastard." I stomped my foot. "I tried, but you've pushed me to it!" So angry I could spit nails, I exploded from this pathetic form into a geyser of water and glared at him. My words reverberated with the depths of my raw power. "Do as I say, or I shall see Olympus destroyed. You have three days, and then you are all gone. So I say. So it is decreed."

A tsunami eighty stories high rolled through the confines of his chambers, sweeping the disgusting creatures away from me. Zeus was sputtering, slamming thunderbolts at my side, but I swatted them away.

"You are nothing, nothing to me, you fool! Today I rain fire. Tomorrow earth. And the day after that, I shall scatter you to the seas, a fate you shall never recover from. Send Hermes to me when you change your mind."

Then, giving him one final, mighty shove, I returned to my home, to my sex slave.

All things considered, I thought I'd handled that affair rather well.

"Two points for Calypso. I think I deserve a gold star today."

Chapter 16

Themis

"Father, what do you expect me to do?" I sidestepped a flaming disk of molten magma that punched a hole through his walls, nearly knocking the head from my body.

When Calypso had threatened to destroy us, she'd meant business. Apollo's home had taken the worst of it; I did not envy that man. Whatever he'd done to her, he'd earned her lifelong wrath for it.

"I expect you to make that bitch stop!" he roared.

Father had been in a horrible mood for the past night. The moment she'd left, the skies had rained fire.

Calypso couldn't control fire, which made this Fiera's doing, and I had to hide my grin. I'd never expected her to speak with her sisters. How she'd corralled them into doing her bidding utterly fascinated me.

"I can't. You know this. She is a Primordial and far beyond our control or punishments."

I could feel his wrath burning holes through me. There were times I was grateful to be blind.

"Judge that man! Send Hades straight to Tartarus."

I notched my chin. "The hand of justice is my own. Only I can sentence him and only I can weigh his sins. My decision has not yet been determined."

"Damn you, girl," he spat. "If I should discover you to be in cahoots with—"

I crossed my arms. "Father, are we done here? I've much left to do before sentencing."

Actually, I had nothing left to do but wait him out. If my wretched father didn't suspend this ridiculous hearing, I would be forced to judge Hades. My last play was the hope that Calypso's threats would change the heart of a rather hardhearted people. I didn't hold out much hope, but as long as there existed even a shred of it, I'd wait this out as long as it took.

"Get out of my sight," he snapped.

Turning on my heel, I made to leave when suddenly I felt the shift of magic. No longer did fire light the skies; now the very earth trembled beneath my feet with a violence that made my heart stutter.

Tiera's turn.

Zeus pounded a heavy fist on his armrest as his beautiful castle began to crumble around his feet.

Hades

"Thalassa," I murmured in her ear.

She slept in my arms, hadn't moved a muscle the entire night. Last night, she'd crawled onto my body, pressed a tender kiss to my chest, whispered a sleepy "mine," and then lost herself to Hypnos's touch.

I'd been unable to keep from spying on her yesterday. There'd been a point in time when I'd not been able to see her at all and had lost her to a void of darkness, to a place where none but the most ancient of peoples could dwell and no one could enter without seeking audience first. But after seeing her threaten Zeus and seeing the shower of rain, I knew she'd gone to speak with her sisters.

Stroking her bare back, I gazed down upon her. She looked so very human today.

Her skin was flesh, her hair blond. And she was snoring.

I chuckled.

"How is it that I've gone all my life without knowing you, my Thalassa?"

Mumbling, she smacked her lips and wiggled her exquisite bum against my thigh. I hungered for her, but I found that I always did anymore. In a matter of days, the woman had grown vital to me, necessary.

Even if her threats didn't work and I was exiled, I would return for her. Oftentimes in the Underworld, when a day had been particularly trying, I'd somehow always found myself at the river Lethe, admiring the supple beauty of its movements, always so feminine to me. Talking to it, telling it my deepest secrets, sharing of myself with those waters in a way I did with no other.

And always I was renewed by the time I'd finished, as though I'd spoken not with water but with a lover who knew my heart and treasured it.

Threading her hair through my fingers, I whispered, "I once called myself master over you, but it is I held thrall by you, mistress of the deep. I am wholly lost to you. And deep down in my soul, I think I always was. I just needed time to learn it."

Her sudden snap of movement blinded me, in an instant she had a leg tossed over my hip and was beaming down at me. "Aw, Death Boy, do you really mean it?"

"Witch!" I chuckled. "You were never asleep."

"Well." She squinted and then grinned. "I was until about an hour ago, but you made such a fine pillow that I had no wish to move, and then Nim told me that lovers liked to whisper sweet nothings in your ear when you were asleep, so I decided to test the theory."

"And how did I do?" I scooted so that I was resting more comfortably against a pile of pillows, which also happened to cause her warm center to slide right over me.

Her eyes sparkled as she ahh'd. "Mmm." She tossed her head back, swaying on me like a gentle tide, her movements so sensuous that I found myself already clenching my teeth from my need to release.

"Isn't it my day?" she mewled, clawing at my chest with her nails, but she never stopped.

"I've lost count." I nipped at a finger that came within reach.

Giggling happily, she snatched it back and swatted my chest. "Play nice, you beastly man, or I shall—"

"Oh shut up," leaning up, I took her lips, snatching the words and breath out of her. Then, with a deft move, I reversed our position on the bed so that I was now the one on top.

We'd not had sex like this before, where so much of me touched so much of her. She'd rubbed herself upon me yesterday morning, but I'd been fully clothed. I looked at her eyes, trying to spy any sign that she did not wish this level of intimacy with me yet.

She wrapped her arms around my neck and grunted, "I'm not getting any younger, beast."

And I settled in. Moving slowly, languorously. Finding a rhythm she liked, nuzzling the side of her neck as her breathy hum filled my ears. And then I'd stop moving and kiss her instead, licking and nipping my way across her body.

"The hollow of your throat tastes like the sweetest of honey," I murmured, laving my tongue along the delicate flesh, delighted to witness a rush of goose bumps raise up on her skin.

"Tell me more," she sighed, running her fingers through my hair.

Hiding my grin against her shoulder, I bit down gently and hefted a breast in my hand.

"What does that feel like to you?" she asked me breathily.

Plucking at her burgeoning nipple, I glanced up at her. Her skin was flushed with dew. Blue eyes gleaming like jewels stared back at me.

"Like a ripe, heavy pomegranate."

Most days she'd prefer a form with larger breasts, but today she was more nubile, with smaller, perkier breasts. It mattered naught to me either way.

"You and your fruit," she said and then exhaled when I resumed suckling her nipple.

"Sweet. So very sweet," I whispered between heated nibbles.

Her leg rubbed up and down my calf.

"I love it when you fill me, Hades. I swear I can see stars when you're inside me."

I chuckled. That had probably been the most sensible thing she'd ever uttered, and still it made me smile. Her innocence was refreshing. None of what I did hadn't already been done to her before, and yet somehow she still behaved as though it were the first time.

Pulling out of her completely so that I could now rest my arms on either side of her thighs, I kissed my way around her navel.

Her fingers moved through my hair, and with a deft twist, she pulled my head up.

"I know where you are headed, lover, so allow me to expedite this process, shall I? You may proceed to my honey hole with the utmost of haste."

I should tell her no for being such an impatient wench? But I wanted nothing more than to be there myself.

With a groan, I abandoned myself to the pleasures of sampling a woman, my woman. In all my time with Persephone, I'd not been chaste. I'd bedded nymphs, satyrs, maidens, centaurs, and others, but only ever to satisfy a carnal craving.

None of us had ever wanted more, but there was something to be said about getting to experience this form of intimacy with one to whom your heart belonged to so completely.

"Gods," she moaned, and I could tell she was close, because her little talons were digging into the back of my neck with a fierceness. But I would not let her come, not yet.

Pulling back, I crawled up her body.

Her eyes were twin flames of fury. "You get your sweet ass back there and finish me off, Death Boy, or—"

But I'd learned how to tame the shrew. I took her lips. And her tongue slid along mine passionately, tasting the essence of her on me. She was vast and endless and created a hunger in me never to be assuaged.

Ready for my own release, I slipped deep inside her and rumbled, "Come when you are ready, my Thalassa."

She fractured in my arms not a second later, dragging me down into the briny depths with her.

Calypso

I took a bite out of my bowl of fresh watercress salad with pickled seamelon, mentally applauding myself for yet another masterful creation—although it would have tasted even better with just a hit of fresh mint on it. I'd have to remember that next time I made it for Nim.

"So you never did say how things are going with the lawyer."

I'd tried my damnedest not to think about Olympus or Olympians in particular for the past day and a half. Already I could feel the tremors of Tiera's powers waning, soon to give way to Aria's winds.

I was sick to my stomach that Zeus was going to ride this out. I mean, I would destroy him, him and all his cronies, but my poor sex slave would still be judged and condemned. And once Themis passed sentence, it could not be undone, not even if I snatched up Persephone and showed her off to her adoring public. Themis's verdict was absolute and final. I was glad justice was on my side, but I was extremely unhappy with how obdurate her prick of a father was being.

Stabbing a fork into my lettuce, I growled, "Not well."

She frowned. "Is there anything Sircco and I can do for him, Janita?"

Releasing my fork so that it clattered back into the bowl, I sighed, hanging my head in my hands. "You've done more than enough for me, truly. The lawyer has done all she can to see the matter resolved, but unless the prosecutor drops his case, there is little I can do to change things."

Nim nodded. "I see."

"I've done my part. And I was surprisingly very calm about it all, level-headed and adult."

Shrewd eyes narrowed. "Did you threaten to raze their town?"

"Of course I did!" I grumped, chuckling at how well she knew me. "But it's mostly a bluff. I'm doing all I can to ensure Henry doesn't see his day in court, but, I feel mostly helpless. This is a feeling I'm struggling with."

Standing from her spot at the head of the table, Nimue got up and waddled over to me and gave me a hard hug.

"I'm sure *Henry*," she stressed his name and chuckled, "will be fine. You always seem to have a knack for figuring out even the hardest of problems. Have a little faith, Janita." Her fingers brushed my cheeks.

"Faith," I scoffed. "In what?"

I was sick to my stomach about all this, and even sex with Hades didn't keep me as happy as it had. I just wanted to know this was over already, no more wondering or worrying.

"In Calypso's magic"—she whispered and I froze, glancing up at her with wide eyes—"for I feel her favor all over you."

"You do?" I asked slowly.

"Oh, she loves you, Janita. She'd be a fool not to. You're quite possibly the most perfect creature, with the exception of Calypso herself—"

"Of course." I tipped my head graciously.

"How could she resist you? I know I can't."

Getting up from my seat, I enveloped my daughter-in-law in a tight squeeze and whispered in her ear, "If I were her, I'd tell you she loves you back."

Her fingers dug into my back and she nodded. "Well if you do ever happen to stumble across her, let her know that I'd not mind a visit from her now and again."

I frowned. The one time I'd shown myself to Nim as I truly was, she'd seemed terrified of me. I'd never wanted to frighten her like that again. But if she really wanted to see the real me, I'd drop by. Now and then.

"I'll let her know." I sniffed, feeling a strange wetness gathering behind my eyelids. I'd say it was tears, but a goddess never wept. "If I should ever happen to see her, that is."

With promises to see one another in the morning, I packed up the basket of food and made for home. Once out of sight of their castle, I shifted to legs, wishing to be bipedal today.

Hades loved to tickle my toes. In fact, he always seemed to find one reason or another to touch my feet, but he'd done the same with my tail, massaging oils into the scales and whispering naughty, naughty things into my ear as he'd done so.

Just thinking about him made me hawt. But then the heaviness of spirit gripped me once again. Aria's assault would be mighty, but so had Fiera's and Tiera's, and not a peep from them.

I gnashed my teeth, debating whether I should just go peek up there, see how things were going, get a feel for the land, as they say.

Suddenly the waters around me turned a rich pink with veins of gold, and I face I hadn't expected to see soon materialized beside me, floating on an ocean current, with no body attached. Aphrodite's beautiful face was smudged with dirt, debris, and soot. Her blond hair was a wild mass, and though she looked harried and unkempt—so unlike her typical self—her megawatt smile was firmly in place.

"Good gods, have you done it now!" She chortled, filling my seas with effervescence.

I frowned. "Done what exactly?"

I was too afraid to hope this might actually be good news.

"Zeus is in a tizzy." Her head bobbed happily. "An absolute tizzy. My poor little Hephy cannot keep up with his constant demand for more lightning. The gods are infuriated with you, Calypso. You've made mighty enemies."

I shrugged. I'd made worse. "Tell me something I don't know."

"Okay." She blinked. "How about the fact that Demeter herself has gone to Zeus and demanded he make this right, no matter the cost."

I gasped, starting to get excited despite myself. "She didn't. Even thinking Hades had murdered her only daughter?"

Dite nodded. "Oh, she did. And when Zeus threatened to strike her down with a bolt, she smacked him. Right there before gods and country. His cheek glistens a bright cherry red even now."

I chortled. I simply couldn't help myself. The supposed offense had been with Demeter, and yet even so, Zeus was refusing to back down. It let me know that my assumptions had been entirely correct. None of this had anything to do with Persephone at all; it was just another one of Zeus's mad grabs for power.

"That bastard of a whore."

"I would laugh, but I probably shouldn't. He is Daddy Dearest, after all." She snickered anyway.

The Olympian family tree was a convoluted hodgepodge of incest and rape, rather fascinating and all very highly disturbing. I tried not to rustle those branches often.

"Anywho, I hear Hephy calling to me. My poor little, twisted man. I will leave you now, Calypso, but know this: he will break. And sooner rather than later. Even Uncle Dearest isn't quite the brownnoser he normally is. There is tell of his waters heaving with the beginnings of birth pains." She laughed. "Remind me never to get on your bad side, Caly."

So Psycho was turning on Master. How very interesting. I snorted. "Not to worry, Dite. You entertain me. I promise that if I do drown the Olympians, I'll spare you, Hephy, and the delightful Themis."

Bobbing her goodbye, she poofed out of existence, and I suddenly felt ten times lighter, as though I were Atlas and the weight of the world had just been tossed from my shoulders. Beaming brightly, I flashed myself to Hades' room and his waiting arms.

He was as he usually was, lying on the bed, nibbling on a tray of cheeses and nuts and reading a book. He had a very dark, sexy nerd appeal to him when he did that. It drove me wild.

Yanking the tale of Oliver Twist from his hands, I tossed the first-edition treasure over my shoulder and kissed him.

"It's happening, Death Boy, the tide is turning. Tomorrow you'll have your pardon."

There wasn't much talk for a while after that, and what was said was mostly, "Mm, right there. Oh yeah, just like that. Or," my personal favorite, "I'm coming!" By the time we'd finished, I was nothing but a heap of goo in his arms.

Hades lazily toyed with my nipple, popping it in and out of his mouth.

"Does that bring you pleasure, sex slave?" I asked him with a voice grown hoarse from too much yelling.

He shrugged, "Always."

"Well then, you may continue." I flicked my fingers, sighing happily as he continued to gently explore my body.

I ran my fingers through the supple ends of his hair, looking up at the ceiling of the room, simply happy to be alive.

I frowned when I noticed he'd not been touching me for the past few minutes. Looking over at him, I shook my head.

His eyes were intense and molten, running across my flesh so that it felt like he was memorizing each and every nuance of me.

"Hades?"

"How can I leave you? Even winning back my freedom, I have enjoyed my enslavement, my goddess."

I chuckled. "I wasn't much of a warden, I fear. I went far to easy on you." I pinched his backside hard.

But he didn't laugh as he normally would.

"Darling?" I crawled out from under him and sat up, worried by the frown lines on his head. "What is it?"

"You are of the waters, Thalassa, and my home is up there. In the Above. I must return."

"I grant you permission to stay. You'll have free rein in my kingdom. You should not want for—"

"But I cannot run the Underworld as I should down here, not permanently."

He'd done a fine job of it since he'd been here, and I said so.

Shoving blunt-tipped fingers through his hair, mussing it even further, he leaned back on an elbow, cocking up one knee in a relaxed yet thoughtful pose.

He truly was a beautiful man, even with the plethora of scars marring his body. There was a light dusting of hair on his legs that I now scratched against with the toe of my foot. I'd never imagined I'd enjoy the feel of coarse hair, but I did his.

He reached for my foot with an absentminded air. Hades was as addicted to my touch as I was to his. I knew this. But I also sensed that his concerns troubled him tremendously.

"You've done a good enough job of it, lover. What need have you to return? Could you not at the least stay for a little while longer?"

"The Styx is flooding, Thalassa. Charon is up to his eyes in dead, and with nowhere to put them, soon the pathways will be bogged down. I have to return. I have souls to weigh and judgment to pass. Come with me?"

He squeezed my foot.

But even as he asked it, I knew I could not be a permanent resident at his home, either. The waters of the world were my own, with the exception of Psycho's little oasis, which I never ventured into. There was much I had to do here, too. Mind the creatures, see to their well-being, ensure a fertile crop for Nim and Sircco.

Those concerns, while valid, were far from the most important, however. I had grandchildren due any day now. I could hardly leave Nimue yet. Not without ensuring the protection of and blessings for my babies first.

"I can't." I shook my head.

His lips twisted, and he released my foot. I felt horribly bereft without his touch. But I wasn't sure whether I should crawl over to him and demand he put his hand back on me or make a joke to lighten the mood.

So instead I did neither.

He slept fitfully that night, hugging tight to me the entire time. We were a pretzel of limbs, clinging like octopus tentacles one to the other. I felt a heaviness in my chest that felt an awful lot like tears.

Goddesses didn't cry, but right then, I could have sworn something wet slid down my nose.

Chapter 17

Hades

I awoke the next morning, and Thalassa (as was her way) was long gone. Scrubbing a hand down my face, I glanced out the window, sensing in my dark soul that today would be my final time getting to gaze upon Seren's unusual dawn.

It seemed to me to be far more beautiful than any dawn I'd seen before it. The colors were a little brighter, the creatures a little more varied and exotic. There were snails with long, feathery tails trailing behind them, fish that looked more like dogs and cats chasing one another, dolphins and their pups chattering among themselves with their high-pitched squeals.

Standing and feeling every one of my more than five thousand years of age, I stretched my arms above my head. No matter what came this morning, I was prepared.

I could feel the powerful tremors running amok through Olympus, the rage of my brothers as they tried to stem the tide of Calypso's fury, to no avail.

My lips twitched. I would miss her more than words could ever express. And though I'd be bound to my lands, I would never forget her. My home would forever remain open to her.

Heavy of spirit and wanting to get on with my day, I shuffled over to handle my morning necessaries. I was just running a comb through my hair when I felt the pop of magic flow through the waters.

Recognizing it as Calypso's morning feast, I hummed under my breath as I walked out. I craved the lemony scones she served me, little dollops of honey on their tops, with a pot of tea. Breakfast was quickly becoming my favorite meal of the day.

But I stopped short the moment I spied the serving table, empty save for one pomegranate that'd been split down the middle, its red, plump seeds glistening and beckoning me forward.

There was nothing around the fruit save for six seeds she'd picked out.

My heart hammered wildly, recognizing immediately the significance of what she'd done.

Legend had it that for the price of eating just six seeds, Persephone's fate had been sealed. Because I'd shared my food with her, now her soul and body belonged to me six months out of the year.

All fabrications, of course; I'd done no such thing. But Calypso was doing just that. With these seeds, I'd be pledging myself to her six months out of every year.

The tempestuous goddess would never let me out of that agreement, either. Once done, this could never be undone. One thing I'd learned from my time with the Sea was that while she was steadfast and true, she was also incredibly possessive.

I had my obligations to my people; I could never leave my home unattended for months at a time. After even just two weeks away, I felt the burden of all that waited for me. But I'd be damned if I'd walk away willingly from her offer.

I thought of all the gods who'd paired up over the course of many lifetimes. Most of them were still together, but none of them were faithful to each other.

Clenching my jaw, I stared at the pearly seeds with a sense of trepidation. I wanted this with Calypso. In fact, I don't think I'd ever wanted anything more.

Persephone had been an ideal quickly shattered when the reality had made itself known. But I knew Calypso. Or I hoped I did.

What if she tired of me?

What if I tired of her?

I sighed, curling my fingers against my pant leg as I took a step forward. Was it possible that she and I could become something wholly set apart from the rest of them? Could we become like one of my humans who, even in death, remained true and ever devoted?

"Screw it," I growled, taking those final steps to the table. I snatched up the seeds, and popped them all in my mouth, chewing and swallowing without hardly tasting them.

But instead of feeling cold and shaking from the enormity of the action I'd just committed, I felt warmth spread through my limbs. Felt the rightness of that action.

I didn't need to glance up to know she was back in the room with me, but I did anyway.

Thalassa was a thing of wild beauty, a towering enchantress with limbs made of water, a face that seemed cut from the finest of crystal, and hair that billowed behind from a swift-moving current. Clinging to her tight little body was a gown made up hundreds of thousands of living creatures in miniature. Her smile glowed.

Never taking her eyes off me, she seemed to float over to table, and without saying a word, she picked out six additional seeds. My heart thundered through my ears like the majestic, fearsome hooves of my Death steeds as she popped them into her mouth and chewed.

As I'd just promised her six months of fealty, now too had she done so to me. I wet my lips, unsure if I understood this completely.

Twin arcs of cascading rainbows hovered over her form, encasing her in a miasma of colors and making me suddenly aware of the very breadth and scope of her powers. This was the Sea. The very waters of life stood before me, and I could do nothing but bow to her.

When I stood back up, she opened her mouth, to say what, I wasn't sure. Because suddenly the waters parted, rolled away to reveal a very beleaguered Hermes.

There were dark circles under his eyes, and his skin was washed out, his hair poking straight up as though he'd been running fingers through it constantly.

The only things that still had a pep to them were his golden winged shoes, which were flapping furiously. Genuflecting before Thalassa, he murmured, "Calypso and Hades, Zeus requests the honor of your appearances. How should I answer his entreaty?"

Sighing deeply, Calypso nodded. "Tell him we're coming."

Jaw clenching, Hermes nodded once and then popped out of there. She looked back at me.

"Hades, this conversation isn't over yet."

Then she grabbed my hand, and we headed to Olympus together.

Calypso

He'd eaten the seeds. I wanted to crow. I wanted to sing. I wanted to hump his cock until I screamed with release.

But I could do none of those things, because Zeus had finally come to his senses.

Walking through the ruined halls of a once-magnificent home, I could hardly believe the destruction before me.

Hades leaned in to whisper in my ear, "Thalassa, I am humbled that you should—"

I stopped walking, forcing him to stop as well, and turned into him. He draped his arms around my waist, and I leaned into him.

"Stop, you hear me? Don't say anything else. I did this, and I would do it again if it meant saving you from his petty schemes. You did not deserve what they planned for you, and I would have no honor if I hadn't stood my ground on this matter."

His fingers strummed my back in a most delicious way. I didn't want to be here. In fact, once we were done here, I'd never again grace the halls of this temple. I was decided. I'd had more than enough of Zeus's fat face to last me a lifetime.

"Stay with me," he said urgently. "When I'm released, choose to stay with me, Thalassa. I have so much work to do, I cannot leave, but I cannot bear to be without—"

I kissed his lovely lips, stealing his words as he often stole mine. I found the use of lips and tongues to be an effective method for silencing a conversation I had no desire to partake in.

There were matters I myself needed to attend to. But I had plans for my dark Under Lord, plans that would take at least twenty lifetimes to complete.

The whisper of his breath passed through me, and he tasted of heat, fire, and dark nights.

I would miss him desperately.

"Let's go speak to Horse Face and get this over, sex slave. You have an Underworld to take care of."

He clenched his jaw, nodded once, and stepped out of my arms, pulling us toward Zeus's chambers.

I sighed.

Most of the temple had fallen down at this point. There were a few walls that'd managed to remain upright, but the majority of them were peppered with massive, darkened holes. The kind of holes that came from fiery rocks flying through the skies.

There'd be a fruit basket in my sisters' futures—but none for Tiera, as the wench had cost me my loveliest Seren Stone.

When we stepped into the chamber, Zeus was sitting on his throne looking regal, clean, and rather kingly. I very reluctantly admitted that last part.

Blue eyes pierced me like volts of electricity. If he could have killed me with a glance, I do believe he'd have been tempted to try.

And surrounding him was the might of the Pantheon. Oh, yawn. As if I couldn't take them down with a flicker of my wee pinky. Gnats.

Aphrodite stood to the left side of her father, fighting a grin and fidgeting on her heels. She didn't wave a greeting, but her obvious effervescence was as good as one.

Themis stood in the center of the room, holding her scales and dressed in the traditional garb of a judge with a white sash tied around her eyes. Her smile was directed straight at me.

I didn't care about the others; they were mostly all busy glaring hate at Hades and me. I sidled next to him until our hips touched, and I smirked.

There was one person, though, that I did feel a twinge of sadness for. Demeter stood off by herself, looking at neither of us. She held her arms around herself, forlorn. As a mother myself, I understood the pain of a child's loss.

"Calypso," Zeus's voice thundered, causing the marble floor beneath us to tremble. "Goddess of the Waters, we ask that you would..."

He swallowed thickly, and I wanted to squawk with laughter. The douchebag did not want to do what he had to do.

"Yes, Zeusy?" I asked sweetly. "What is it you wish to say to me?"

Fingers tap-tapping impatiently on this golden throne's armrest, he turned his face to the side. Hades squeezed my fingers.

I wasn't sure if he was asking me to tone down my enthusiasm or merely giving me his strength, but I patted his hand. I had myself well in hand. I would not embarrass him. I had the gods where I wanted them and had no further need to humiliate them.

Not even Apollo uttered a word. Psycho was busy picking at his nails. Athena, Artemis, no one made a sound. At the very least I'd reminded the fools who I was.

I might remain placid and in the background of their lives, but there were beings much more powerful than them out there, and every so often, it was good to eat a little bit of meek pie.

No wait, that hadn't sounded right.

With an angry huff, Zeus scowled and said with a rapidity that blurred his words together, "Forgive us our temerity, elemental, we only wish to remain friends."

Clapping my hands, I slipped my fingers together and gathered my hands to my breast. "Aw, Zeusy, how sweet. Well, of course I forgive you. Forgiven and forgotten." I dusted my hands and flicked my fingers. "And I think it's good we should get this nasty business behind us."

His nostrils flared.

The chamber grew heavy with tense silence. Zeus had once again turned his face to the side. He was dragging this out. I'd forget all about my temporary ceasefire without assurances of Hades' freedom, though, and he knew it.

I tapped my foot, waiting. I was a patient woman; I could wait hundreds of thousands of years to carve out walls from rocks and shape the lands to my whim. But Zeus simply pushed all my "I hate you buttons." It was hard not to crush him with my fist right now.

But finally, *finally* the ugly cow looked at my lover.

"Hades, all charges against you have been dropped. It seems we were in the wrong after all. You may return to your post immediately."

Then, with a clap of his hands that rolled like thunder, Zeus vanished. Probably to go nurse his wounds, big fat baby.

I stuck out my tongue at the empty throne, lifted a brow at Apollo when he opened his mouth as though he wished to speak, and then chortled when he wisely decided to follow El Capitan's lead and scram.

All but Themis, Aphrodite, and Demeter vanished.

And Demeter stayed only because I refused to let her leave. I'd frozen her in a tower of water. She glared at me.

Hades clenched my fingers as I made to walk forward.

"What are you going to do, Thalassa?"

I held up a finger. "I wish to speak with her, lover. Do not leave before I come back.

Lifting my chin, I glided toward Demeter in all my goddessy glory. Her brown eyes, while angry, still glowed with the ghost of pain.

I sighed and, reaching through the pillar of water, grabbed her hand, holding fast to it.

"De, listen to me. None of this was done to hurt you. Please understand that. I wish you to know something. Persephone is well. She lives."

The anger in her eyes was suddenly replaced with hope. "She lives?"

"Yes, Goddess of the Harvest. She does. But your daughter is wild and, unchecked, she has grown even more so. Hades placed her at a location where she is being kept safe and far from harm. I personally ensured that this is so."

My words rang with the conviction of truth, a truth she felt through every fiber of her soul. As one mother to another, I would never lie to her about something like that.

"Can I see her?"

"No." I shook my head. "Not yet. But she will be released come spring as she always is. And hopefully this time, a little wiser for her time spent away. I tell you this so you can retain your hope and faith, not so you can try to find her or accuse Hades of any more treachery. If you cross me, I will know, and the hell you've experienced these past three days will be nothing to the hell I'll bring upon you and your house. You have a kind soul, Demeter, but you did your daughter a grave disservice raising her as you did."

I would probably never win mother of the year, but I'd have slapped Sircco or Sirenade silly if they'd ever treated another with the utter disdain and disrespect Persephone had shown Hades time and time again.

"It is hard to tell my daughter no."

I shrugged. "But sometimes that's the best thing to do—tell them no. Set boundaries. Let them know their limitations and that you mean business if they cross them. She may be eternally youthful, but she is no child. Do not treat her as one. You may go." I flicked my wrist, dropping the wall of water, but before she could leave, I imparted one final truth to her. "And as to Persephone cohabitating with Hades for half of the year, that is at an end. No more. Sex Stick belongs to me."

And since that was all there was left to say, I turned my back on her and walked back to Hades.

He merely smiled, reaching for me immediately and wrapping me up tight in his embrace.

Themis and Dite stood beside him.

"What. What." Dite lifted her hands in the air and did a shoulder-shrugging dance. "We did it. Let it never be said that a woman can't change the world. Because girls, we pretty much just pulled off the impossible."

Themis and I laughed heartily.

"That we did," she said sweetly. "It was truly an honor conspiring with you, goddess." Themis bowed deeply. "And remember, my cave is always open to you."

I inclined my head. "I know."

With a chuckle, she vanished. But Dite remained just a moment longer. She glanced between us and sighed.

"I see great things in your future. A power to be reckoned with. I don't think Zeus or Psycho—" she winked at me, and I giggled "—will ever attempt another coup of your realm, Hades. Not with your new guard dog at your heels."

"Pft." I flicked my wrist. "I am at no man's heels. He rests at mine. Don't you, sexy?" I winked.

He squeezed me tight.

"Okay then." Dite shrugged. "It's been swell. You kids have fun, stay safe, and don't ever change for the world. Oh, I just adore you guys! You're like my new super team." Aphrodite vanished with a sparkle of light.

I turned to Hades. It was just him and me now.

"Thalassa?" He groaned.

And I knew what he wanted, what he was asking me. But I couldn't leave. Not yet.

Leaning up on tiptoe, I kissed him. "I adore you, Death Boy. We'll see each other soon, I promise."

It was an ache when with a final nod, he hugged me tight, and then he too left me.

I stood in the center of that ruined hall, staring up at the azure skies, and this time, I did cry.

Chapter 18

Hades

It'd been a month since I'd seen or held Thalassa last. I'd hoped in vain that she would come to me at some point. Every night I visited the Lethe, speaking my truth to it. Imagining that somehow she was listening, that she heard me.

But not once had she replied.

Tonight was the final time I'd return to these shores. I stared at the sparkling waters under the midnight moon, remembering the moments we'd spent together, the two weeks that'd felt like both an eternity and no time at all, and shook my head.

"I miss you, Thalassa, each day, each night. My realm feels empty without you in it. I cannot fault you for remaining where you are. How could I, when I am forced to do the same?"

I closed my eyes as a gentle breeze rolled through, bringing with it the scent of roses, a flower I would now and forevermore associate with my goddess. I'd eaten the seeds and so had she. We'd pledged our souls—one to the other. I was bound to her eternally, but I ached, ached for what we couldn't have again.

"You idiot."

My eyes snapped open, and I gazed on in open-mouthed wonder as Thalassa walked across the water toward me. She wore a gown of sheer amethyst that sparkled like its namesake. Her soft green hair was piled high on her head, and twined through it was a riot of sea rose buds.

"So quick to give up on me? I see how it is." She flicked at my shoulder when she finally stepped foot on land.

Grunting incoherently, I snatched her up, wrapping her in my arms, pretty sure I would never release her again.

"Oomph," she hissed, banging on my chest, "Death Boy, can't breathe."

I eased my hold a little. A very little.

Just enough so she could worm her arms up and frame my face. Her touch moved through my body like liquid, burning me up from the inside with a crazed sort of fever.

"Thalassa, how, I thought—"

Rubbing noses with me, she laughed, and I swear the Elysian night sang with the sound of it. From the corner of my eye, I caught sight of ghostly faces peeking out from behind the thick trunks of trees, staring at me in wonder.

I'd always been known as the broody god. To hear my laughter now must have terrified them.

"Did you think I put out those seeds for nothing, dill bag? I meant what I said when I ate them. You're mine, and I'm yours, and yada yada yada. Six months out of the year, we swap back and forth, every night. I had time to think about this, Bubble Butt, and we can still run our kingdoms and keep our nights to ourselves. I mean, honestly, what could possibly go wrong at bedtime?"

I lifted a brow. In our world, everything could go wrong.

"Okay, okay." She wagged her hand. "Forget that. So the world could come crashing down around our feet. Big deal. We'll rebuild, start over. We'll do whatever we need to do, but I can't do this separation thing anymore. I'm not built for this. Do you know how many times I've had to pleasure myself—"

I growled. "No one may pleasure you but me. Not even your own hands are allowed down there unless I am present."

She giggled, wiggling her lower body on my painful hardness. "Yes, Master."

Groaning, I ran my hands over her bare back, ready to tear this flimsy fabric off her gorgeous body and have my way with her.

"Hades, guess what," she squealed, eyes shining with what looked suspiciously like tears.

I paused in my exploration of her. "What?"

"We're grandparents! Oh, you have to meet my little darlings, Uriah and Fable, they're so precious and adorable and have my eyes and my hair and my little nose and—"

"Are you sure you did not birth them yourself, my love?"

She snorted. "Don't be silly. But tomorrow, you shall come to meet them."

"And tonight?" I asked with heat filling my words.

Her smile was pure wickedness as she said, "Tonight I brought carrots."

Epilogue: 500 years later

Calypso

Today was the twins' five hundredth birthday, and I wanted the babies to have a very special one. So I'd snuck them over to play with Cere while I set up their birthday tent in Elysia.

Themis glanced around, her hands on her hips, and nodded expertly. "Yes, I think this will do, Caly. You've got a dragon for Uri and a Pegasus for Fable."

"Yes, yes." I batted her words away. "But have you seen the pile of cupcakes I made? I learned from the master chef in Wonderland, a girl by the name of Alice who showed me that if you dipped the fruit in choco—"

"Eeeps!" Dite squealed, clapping her hands merrily the moment she materialized beside us. "Look at this place. Oh, the darlings are simply going to love it."

"Dite." I gave her a stern look. "You would show up at the last minute. Heffer, do your thing. You know we can't get this party started without it."

Beaming like the proud aunt she was, she nodded. "Yes, ma'am."

Then, with an air kiss, she released her magic to the breezes, causing the night sky to dance with tiny jeweled lights that bobbed and glimmered like lightning bugs. I busied around in the tent, making sure the placement of the gifts was just so on the table.

I patted Linx's tank. She hated coming to the Above, but my sister refused to miss the twins' party. Neighing softly, she contented herself with munching on the jeweled candy grass Hades had crafted for her and flicked her tail happily.

Nim and Sircco would show up later. I'd warned the boy to wear his legs tonight, but I was sure he wouldn't. For some reason he still detested the use of them. So, just to be on the safe side, I'd turned half of Elysia into a large wading pool so the maidens and he would feel comfortable here.

A strong pair of arms slipped around my waist, and the rumble of my man's voice whispered in my ear. "Have I ever told you just how sexy you look when you're acting all domestic?"

Twirling, I smacked his chest and laughed. "Hm. Why don't you tell me that again." I wiggled my hips against him.

Even after all these years, we still mated like rabbits. I'd come to the conclusion that I would never get my fill of this beastly man.

"Down, beast, down," Aphrodite cried laughingly, sidling up next to us. "We have guests. Let's keep this PG since there are kids present now."

Sighing, I patted his cheek as he pouted. "No worries, my love, I've a field full of carrots just waiting for you."

"Thalassa," he growled, and then he shook his head and chuckled. "Woman, you will be the death of me."

I snorted. "Not hardly, Bubble Butt."

Then with a wave and a la-de-da, I walked over to greet the guests. Young and old, ghosts, mortals, maidens, Nim and my boy Sircco, even my elemental sisters showed up, though Tiera scowled the entire time. But they all came. Dite's little Hephy made an appearance. Grumpy thing that he was, he'd still managed to craft gifts for both Fable and Uri, matching unicorns made of wood.

"All ye need to bring them to life," he said, gazing at the twins, "is to whisper a name in their ear, and they will be forever yours."

Fable, the granddaughter of my very soul, was a dark-skinned, dark-haired beauty with eyes of deepest bronze just like her father's. Her skin was as dark as the deepest depths of an ocean trench and her lips like the reddest of roses. She was heartachingly lovely, and all who knew her loved her. But unlike her rapscallion brother, she'd not been born with the ability to wear a tail.

She accepted the bauble with a humble nod of thanks and hugged it tight to her breast.

"I will cherish it, Hephy." She kissed his cheek, and I didn't think it possible, but the dwarf actually blushed. Then again, Fable had that effect on everyone.

Uriah, whose flesh was an unusually stunning shade of pearlescent sea green and bore a head of shockingly bright and thick blue hair, grinned. He had Sircco's looks, swarthy and devastatingly handsome. And with the pick of any maiden he wanted, the boy knew he was hawt and strutted through Seren like a peacock on the loose.

He was my boy through and through.

"Thanks, homey," he said.

Nimue rolled her eyes. "Uri, that is not how a prince should speak."

Uri, who was always in mischief of one form or another (but whom I secretly adored since he reminded me of me as that age), sighed. "Yes, Mom."

"Uri." Sircco growled a warning at the boy, twin bolts of lightning flaring through his bronze eyes.

Thinning his lips, my devastatingly handsome grandson grumped, "Yes, Dad. Thanks, Hephy," he said.

The dwarf shook his hand then thumped him on the chest and said, "It's nothing, homey."

Then with a wink and a wave, he vanished, and everyone laughed.

"Gods help us," Nimue cried. "How can I teach my wayward child some respect when everyone around us is bound and determined to undermine me?" But she said it with an exasperated chuckle.

Hades leaned in to my side from where we sat at the head of the table beside our grandchildren and said, "This was a wonderful idea to have the party here, my love."

I beamed proudly. "I know. But you want to know what the very best idea is that I've ever had?"

Turning on my seat, I looked at him head on. Even after all this time, my heart still skipped a beat when he was near.

Grabbing my hands, he placed a tender kiss on each palm. "And what's that?"

"The day I decided to make you my sex slave."

He laughed, and the party went into full swing after that. Wine flowed and music blared.

Themis was in charge of the tunes tonight, and I smiled when I heard an upbeat one entirely apropos of how I felt this evening.

The song went something along the lines of "oh, oh, oh, you've got the best of my love."

And yeah, that was pretty much all that needed to be said about that.

"I love you, Death Boy," I whispered.

"And I you, Thalassa, forever, for always, eternally."

"Oh, swoon, you say the sweetest things."

Hades took my lips and well...you know how this story ends. Forever. For always. And eternally.

The End

And never was there a story of more love than that of Calypso, and her dark-souled Romeo...

So I say to you now farewell, dear reader, but do not despair, for I have far greater stories to share of dark queens you thought you knew. Until we meet again...

~Anon, One of the 13 Keepers of the ***Tales****.*

Love my books? Want to know when the next Dark Queen book will be released? Make sure to sign up for my newsletter! And if you really want to get to know more about the queens and all the characters to come, come hang out at the The Harem.

Want some more yummy goodness to read while you wait for the next queen? Then keep turning the pages to catch a sneak peek of Kenzie Cox's awesome shifter serial set in the steamy, lush bayous!

Author's Notes

Once upon a time in a Kingdom far, far away lived an author who wrote fairy tale stories who went by the name Marie Hall. That author and this author are one and the same. So if you happen to spy some characters that seem strangely familiar to you, it's really no coincidence. And if you'd like to read some of Marie's works, stay tuned for a complete listing of all those books.

The next queen is coming soon, though it's a mystery who she'll be. If you want to know, stay tuned to either Jovee Winters's FB page or sign up for her newsletter, which is probably the best way to keep up to date.

The next queens, in no particular order, are as follows:

The Ice Queen
The Dark Queen (Fable's Story)
The Fire Queen (Fiera's Story)
The Magic Queen (Baba Yaga's story)
The Passionate Queen (Based on Red Queen from Wonderland)

About Jovee Winters

Jovee Winters is the pen name of a *NY Times* and *USA Today* bestselling author who loves books that make you think or feel something, preferably both. She's also passionate about fairy tales, particularly twisting them up into a story you've never thought could be possible.

She's married to the love of her life, a sexy beast of a caveman who likes to refer to himself as Big Hunk. She has two awesome kids she likes to call Thing 1 and Thing 2, loves cooking, and occasionally has been known to crochet. She also really loves talking about herself in the third person.

Marie Hall Books

Kingdom Series (Fairy Tale Romance)

Her Mad Hatter (Free everywhere! Book 1, based on Alice and the Mad Hatter)
Gerard's Beauty (Book 2, based on Beauty and the Beast)
Red and Her Wolf (Book 3, based on Little Red Riding Hood)
The Kingdom Collection (Books 1–3, with bonus deleted scenes)
Jinni's Wish (Book 4, based on Arabian Nights)
Hook's Pan (Book 5, Based on Peter Pan)
Danika's Surprise (Book 5.5, novelette and first introduction to the upcoming Dark Princess Series)
Kingdom Chronicles (Books 4 & 5, and includes Danika's Surprise)
Moon's Flower (Book 6, based on the legend of the Man in the Moon)
Huntsman's Prey (Book 7, spinoff Dark Princess Series)
Rumpel's Prize (Book 8, loosely based on the legend of Rumpelstiltskin and Beauty and the Beast)
Hood's Obsession (Book 9)
Her One Wish (Book 10)
A Pirate's Dream (Book 11)

Jace, Mating Season Part 1

In the wilds of the bayou...

Jace Riveaux has wanted her since the first moment she stepped into his bayou bar three years ago. And now she's back, unattached, and ready for the taking. One afternoon together, and he knows she's the one. Only his world is dangerous, he has secrets, and trust is hard to come by...especially when all signs point to her being aligned with his enemy.

Skye Michaels has nothing left to lose. After a bad breakup, she flees to her favorite southern Louisiana town, determined to finally get photographs of the majestic wolves that roam the area. Instead she gets what she really came for—Jace Riveaux. But when the Riveauxs are threatened by someone she knows, suddenly she has more to lose than ever.

Sneak Peek

I stepped back into the oppressive heat and stood on the weathered wooden porch. "Since when is it ever this hot in March?"

He shook his head. "Heat wave." Then his gaze traveled the length of my body, lingering on my bare legs.

I'd chosen a pale yellow sundress that hit a few inches above my knee, but the way he was devouring me with his intense gaze, I was starting to feel like I was wearing nothing but my Victoria's Secret lace. "Umm..."

He raised his gaze to meet mine, a secret smile claiming his lips. "It was my turn."

I pulled my camera from its case and frowned at him. "Your turn for what?"

His smile reached his eyes. "You took your time checking me out. Twice. Don't think I didn't notice. So I did the same. Only I didn't ask you to take your shirt off... yet."

Aiden, Mating Season Part 2

She's the one woman he can't have...

Rayna Vincent has wanted Aiden Riveaux since she was sixteen years old. There's only one problem—he doesn't do relationships. So when he offers her a season of stolen nights with no strings attached, she accepts, willing to take him any way she can... even if she knows her heart will never survive.

Aiden Riveaux has a problem. A big one. He's sleeping with Rayna, his brother's best friend and the girl everyone thought of as his. Aiden knows he's has to break it off, but after one hot night everything's changed, including Rayna. Now she's his. And he intends to keep it that way... no matter what.

Sneak Peek

I slipped into the kitchen to drop off the dirty glasses. On my way back to the bar, Aiden rounded the corner and grabbed my wrist. He pulled me into the storage room and kicked the door closed.

He pressed me up against the wall, one hand clutching my hip as he ran his knuckles gently over my cheek. "You're killing me, Ray."

I raised a skeptical eyebrow, trying to ignore the way my heart was trying to beat out of my chest. "You look plenty alive to me."

"Not for long if I don't get you out of this skirt and your long legs wrapped around my waist."

Oh, God. Lust clouded my brain, and the memory of him fucking me on his kitchen table last week made me clutch at his black T-shirt. I stared up into his hungry gaze. "After work?"

"Now."

Both serial parts now free with Kindle Unlimited!

Made in the USA
San Bernardino, CA
26 November 2018